The Tygrine Cat

The Tygrine Run

Inbali Iserles Inbali Iserles is a lawyer, writer and keeper of exotic rodents. The idea for her first novel, *The Tygrine Cat*, came to her as she leafed through a book on cat breeds and began to imagine a rivalry between ancient feline tribes. *The Tygrine Cat* was highly recommended by The School Librarian and praised as "A spellbinding tale" by Booklist. It won the 2008 Calderdale Children's Book of the Year Award.

A chance discovery on a London street set in motion the theme of Inbali's second novel, *The Bloodstone Bird*, one of The Independent's 50 Best Winter Reads for 2009/2010.

The Tygrine Cat On the Run is the much-awaited sequel to *The Tygrine Cat*.

You can find out more about Inbali at
www.inbaliiserles.com

The Tygrine Cat On the Run

INBALI ISERLES

WALKER BOOKS

First published in Great Britain 2011 by Walker Books Ltd
87 Vauxhall Walk, London SE11 5HJ

2 4 6 8 10 9 7 5 3 1

Text © 2011 Inbali Iserles

The right of Inbali Iserles to be identified as author of this
work has been asserted by her in accordance with the
Copyright, Designs and Patents Act 1988

This book has been typeset in Weiss

Printed and bound in Great Britain by Clays Ltd, St Ives plc

British Library Cataloguing in Publication Data:
a catalogue record for this book is
available from the British Library

ISBN 978-1-4063-2017-6

www.walker.co.uk

for David, with love

And to Chaya, Gisela and Izo –
In the land of memory,
you live for ever

I am not a friend and
I am not a servant.
I am the cat who
walks by himself...

From *Just So Stories* by
Rudyard Kipling

Author's Note

Archaeologists searching for an Egyptian shrine have discovered the remains of two feline tribes: the Sa Mau, spotted cats of the Nile Delta, and the russet-furred Abyssinia Tygrine from ancient Nubia. It is said that the tribes were descendants of Te Bubas, the first cat, and that they wielded magical powers. Some could enter Fiåney, the feline spirit world that existed between wakefulness and sleep. There was a great force to be harnessed in Fiåney – and not all would use it for good.

The Sa embodied cat's killer instinct, the Tygrine her playful spirit. Armed with Fiåney's mysterious powers, the ruthless Sa sought to crush the Tygrine, and condemn all cats to darkness.

Even those who believe the legend claim the tribes became extinct 9,000 years ago with the domestication of cats. They are mistaken…

Prologue

Mati crouches on a hilltop, a hot wind flattening his fur. In the yawning valley below he sees cats like him, with long, narrow limbs and winding tails: legions of russet-furred cats. Their eyes are closed, they purr together, mustering strength from their ancient beliefs. Mati senses their hopes and fears. He hears the murmurs of their voices; they call to Te Bubas, the first cat. They ask her to watch over them.

From his vantage point on the hilltop, Mati sees movement beneath the shimmering sun. The army of the Sa Mau draws nearer. The fighters approach noiselessly, spotted coats scarcely visible against the glaring sand; yet the russet-furred Tygrines sense their presence, open their eyes and stand tall. For a moment, there is silence as the armies pause, eyes locked. Then they charge, the stillness of the air slashed with hisses and caterwauls. The cats clash and roll in the sand – tearing flesh, drawing blood. Sealing a feud so ancient that time has forgotten how it began.

This is the first battle, Mati knows, the ancient battle between the two feline tribes. Spirits still murmur of the epic war between the Tygrine and the Sa. The war that left the Empire of the Abyssinia Tygrine in tatters, that saw his ancestors fall in their thousands. But instead of a Tygrine defeat, Mati sees the russet-furred cats defend the territory proudly. Their angular faces are resolute, their strong jaws set. No flicker of doubt darkens their eyes: right is on their side, and they can only win. They fight in formation, pressing forward, forcing back the army of the Sa Mau. Sand billows in clouds around the sparring armies. Through it, Mati sees the spotted cats glance fearfully over their shoulders. Unlike the Tygrines, their ranks are fraying, giving way to fear and indecision. Several fighters hesitate, overwhelmed by the Tygrines' confidence – by their bold, furious energy. One of the Sa fighters quails, panics; fleeing from the Sa front-line. Another follows.

The Tygrines are on the move, stalking shoulder to shoulder, and the Sa are retreating. Something tangy and delicious catches on Mati's tongue. *Victory*. The Tygrine cats are winning after all. Theirs is the stronger army, the more determined, the better prepared. Mati edges closer to the verge of the hilltop, fur tingling with excitement. His eyes drift towards a small mound of rocks to his right. His ears flick back and he sniffs the dry air. With a curious pang, he longs to draw closer to the rock mound.

Meanwhile, Mati – the same russet-furred cat – sits frozen beneath a market stall at Cressida Lock. People pass whiskers away from him, admiring the jewellery on display, the colourful clothes and savoury snacks. The market cats are also close, wandering beside the bins in the hope of a morsel of meat. But Mati doesn't see them: he is in a trance. His body is in the waking world but his spirit is lost in Fiáney, the magical realm between wakefulness and sleep.

His second self is far from the market-place, far from the stalls and the feral cats. Looking back across history at the bloody scene below, Mati shudders. Something is stirring in the valley through the clouds of sand. Mati sees a dark mass gliding past the Sa fighters. He presses closer to the edge of the hilltop, squinting. Is it a cat? Where this mass moves, darkness grows in clots against the scorching sun, sweeping across the valley like black fire. It reaches over the Tygrine army. One after another, russet-furred fighters drop like broken dolls. The Tygrine formation fractures. Brave warriors launch themselves at the advancing shadow, but to no avail – its lightning-fast claws are like razors, its fangs like shards of splintered glass. The cats collapse in their dozens, golden eyes rolling, legs kicking feebly until they move no more. Their blood sluices into rivulets and sinks into the desert sands where their ghosts will linger for ever.

Mati's second self shrinks from the hilltop. For a moment

his mind drifts and he returns to Cressida Lock, a colourful market-place in a city far from the horrors of a battle long ago. But Fiåney draws him once more. "Come to me, Mati," it calls him. "Come and see... You want to see, Mati. You want to know the truth..."

Mati steps again into the dream-wake. He is staring back through time.

There is nothing to fear, he tells himself: history is the past, and the past cannot touch me.

And so he creeps to the edge of the hilltop, deeper into Fiåney. Despite the throbbing sunshine, the moon appears in the sky, full and deathly pale. Who shall mourn for the Tygrine cat? it whispers. Who shall remember when none are left to grieve?

Mati's eyes scan the valley, tracing the scattered bodies of fallen Tygrines. And there it is, the dark mass, stealing over the sand with unearthly speed. Where it passes there is only death. Suddenly the creature pauses and Mati can see him properly for the first time. He recognizes this cat – he has met him before in Fiåney's shaded corridors. It is the Suzerain, the merciless leader of the Sa Mau. Mati is faint with terror. He watches, trembling, as the Suzerain raises his head, turning his fierce black eyes towards the hilltop.

He can't see me, Mati assures himself. He can't see through time! He can't—

Their eyes meet and the world starts spinning. Mati hears

screaming cats, the crackle of flames, the rumble of thunder.

The Suzerain is reaching through Fiåney, through history – and he is coming for Mati.

The first Gate

A Changing Tide at Cressida Lock

Far away from the desert at the heart of an ancient world, life clustered along the river on Cressida Lock. Insects glided on the surface of the water and buzzed overhead. Pigeons drank and splashed in puddles at the edges of the bank. Fish darted deep within the silty depths. A small, ruddy-brown cat sat gazing at the water, surrounded by tall grass. He thought about the river from his kittenhood – the vast river that spanned the territory of two warring empires. He cocked his head, trying to catch a glimpse of his reflection. His features ebbed and disappeared.

Mati turned back to the market-place that he now called home. It was alive with activity. Humans collected around stalls, playing music and chatting. Food vendors handed out hotdogs, noodles and spicy curries in exchange for paper

19

notes and shiny coins. Several cats hung around nearby, waiting to scavenge morsels of meat that the humans dropped without a glance.

After the confrontation between the local cats and their rivals the Kanks, the two kins had come together to live as friends at Cressida Lock. They were all Cressida Cats now, regardless of where they came from. Things hadn't always run smoothly – a scuffle for a chamber in the catacombs here, a dispute over a hunting ground there. But soon the feral cats had adjusted to the kin's enlarged size. For the most part, they got along.

The kins had joined on the night that Mati fought Mithos, a terrifying cat sent by the Suzerain, high leader of the Sa Mau. Some of the ferals had tried to stop Mithos, to defend the Territory – they had fallen. Mithos had seemed invincible: he could not have been defeated by an ordinary cat. But Mati was no ordinary cat. He was the last in line to the Tygrine throne, gifted with the power to enter Fiåney, the feline dream-wake. Yet he was still only a catling, just out of kittenhood – he barely understood what this meant, scarcely appreciated the beauty and danger of that strange land.

Mati had refused leadership of the Cressida Cats when it was offered to him by Chief Pangur. He was keen to fit in – to be just another street cat. Pangur had agreed but some of the other ferals were uneasy in Mati's presence – still unsure of how to treat him, and what it meant to be a Tygrine.

Mati's eyes trailed towards the deserted part of the market-place. Beyond the bustle of people was the old locked stall where Jess used to live. She had been a housecat who had become lost: a stray. Not like the ferals. They were independent, had always lived in cat-only communities, had never granted socage – that is, comfort and protection to a human in return for food and lodgings. They had never "owned".

Jess had been different. She had owned an old man and had eventually returned to him. Mati knew that this was right – that Jess belonged with this human, who needed her to take care of him. Still, he missed his friend. With a jolt of sadness, he recalled her pretty, tortoiseshell-and-white face and her intense green eyes.

He started towards the park where he'd once met a wise old cat, a shalian called Etheleldra. He had searched for her many times since – for her hollow oak – but she was nowhere to be found. Even now, after several moons on the market-place, Mati could not understand where Etheleldra had gone. He longed to talk to her about his recent journeys into the feline spirit realm. He had seen terrible things in Fiåney – an ancient battle between tribes of cats; the defeat of the Tygrine army; the deathly attack of the cat with the Suzerain's face. Were these images real? Could they be an omen, a warning from loyal spirits that danger lurked in the dream-wake's dark vaults? Were they shards of history – fragments of a distant past?

His mind wandered to the three pillars of cat: *instinct, judgement and spirit*. He knew that the pillars stood for the inherent wisdom that governed all cats, even though most had not heard of them. It was with his knowledge of the pillars that Mati had defeated Mithos, the Suzerain's assassin. But what had happened to the Suzerain? Was the feline overlord out there somewhere? Mati strained for a moment to remember the great battle he had witnessed in Fiåney. The cat in the valley had looked like the Suzerain... Mati's muscles tensed at the thought, and he shivered.

"Yeeeeeoooooow!" yowled a voice behind him and Mati leapt into the air, his fur puffing up instantly. A black-and-white catling sprang on his back, throwing him to the ground. The Tygrine was pinned.

"Surrender, weakling!" hissed Domino.

"Never!" cried Mati. He twisted out of Domino's grip and bolted between the park railings and across the grass, the black-and-white in pursuit. Mati shot towards the fragrant flower-beds, through clouds of violet asters and lilac pansies. His friend dropped behind. Mati glanced over his shoulder. "Last one at the elm is an oolf's snout!"

Being compared to a dog was a terrible insult. Domino picked up pace, charging after Mati. The Tygrine looped back towards the railings, scrambled out of the park and pounced against the towering elm on its border, clutching the bark with small hooked claws. In a moment, Domino was on him and they rolled at the foot of the elm, nipping each other playfully.

"Oolf's snout!" declared Mati.

"*You're* the oolf's snout!" protested Domino, batting the Tygrine's black-tipped tail.

Mati gave a *pirrup*, a trill of pleasure, and stretched his long back legs. It was early autumn but the air remained warm, with seasonal flowers still in bloom. He started to purr. All thoughts of the shadow cat faded beneath the morning sun.

Upstream, near the end of a row of terraced houses where a fishmonger had once lived, two men pulled up in a white van. One hopped out carrying a large metal box with a handle.

A market vendor approached him. "You from the Council?" she asked.

The man nodded. "Pest control. We've been told there are rats in the catacombs, it's a health hazard. It's not like we've had a typical English summer, is it? The rats like the mild weather as much as we do."

"But the market won't be affected, will it?"

"Nah." The man shook his head. "We've put out letters about it so people keep their dogs away. Dogs'll eat anything." The man set the metal box on the ground, pulled on some gloves and reached inside.

The vendor peered over his shoulder. "You're using poison, not traps?"

"Poison's more effective."

The vendor frowned.

"Nothing to worry about," the man assured, "we don't put it just anywhere – down drains, under stalls, that sort of thing." He waved expansively towards the market-place. Beyond the throng of people, a russet-furred cat played with his black-and-white friend. A wind rose across the river and with it a bank of clouds gathered darkly overhead.

The Happy Tuna

Sparrow yawned noisily. "A gastronomic feast to delight the senses!" He licked the last flake of tuna from his whiskers and sat back in his cosy chamber. He tried to reach across his not inconsiderable stomach to groom a patch of mottled fur, but he soon gave up with a grunt.

Mati purred. He had been sharing Sparrow's chamber since his arrival at Cressida Lock. He liked it here. It was true that the old ginger tom talked rather a lot, that he never hunted and that when he was not talking – or eating – he was invariably sleeping. There was nothing wrong in that, thought the catling.

"Where did you find that tuna, Mr Sparrow?"

"That tuna?" Sparrow glanced up for a moment, confused. His pink tongue lapped at his nose. "Ah yes, yes, *that* tuna!

It was a fine cut of fish, was it not?" Sparrow's eyes became dreamy. "My denim lady, of course. How she looks after me, ah, she does take care of her old Sparrow." He started to wash his face with a curved ginger paw. "I have told you the tale of the happy tuna, of course?"

Mati shook his head.

Sparrow froze, tongue out, paw raised. "Well, I..." his words tangled on his tongue. He swallowed. "Well, I can scarce believe I haven't!" He instantly abandoned his wash and struggled into a raised position.

Mati settled down, pleased. A story was on its way, and he planned to relax and enjoy it.

Sparrow cleared his throat. "As you know," he began, "tuna is one of the fastest fishes in the sea."

This, in fact, was news to Mati. He hadn't even realized that tuna came from the sea. He had assumed that they lived in rivers, like the one at Cressida Lock.

"They're big, too!" Sparrow went on. "I mean, we hardly ever see them whole."

It was true that Mati had never spotted anything much larger than a cat's paw darting beneath the murky water of the lock.

"Even that horrible fishmonger rarely had an entire tuna... You remember the fishmonger?" asked Sparrow.

Mati nodded. He remembered only too well. The man had kept a stall on the market-place. He had hated the ferals and had flooded the lock during a thunderstorm to

26

fill the catacombs with water. It had been a lucky escape for the kin. The Cressida Cats had got their revenge, though – they had driven out the fishmonger. But Mati still cringed as he thought about the flood. It was the same night he had found the first robin of the harvest moon, the bird that had died of fright. The other cats had cast him out, accusing him of murder, but Mati had sensed something deadly in the air – he had felt the presence of the Suzerain. And now, sitting in the warmth of Sparrow's chamber, a familiar foreboding sent his fur prickling.

Sparrow was watching him. "My boy, is something wrong?"

Mati shook his head, pushing away these thoughts. "So how big is a tuna?"

"Ah yes," Sparrow continued cheerfully. "Not even that fishmonger had a whole one very often. They can be as big as several felines put together! You wouldn't wish to meet one on a dark night... No... Anyway, this particular tuna had been on a long journey. He had travelled endlessly to find food, only to realize that he was a very, very long way from home. You see, his home was a shallower sort of sea, with baking hot water, and lots of colourful fish. But the tuna, he wasn't anywhere like that... He was in a gigantic ocean, which was so deep it didn't have a bottom, and salty too!" Sparrow wrinkled his nose in disgust.

"Do they really travel such long distances?" said Mati.

"Yes, yes of course! Would I exaggerate?" Sparrow

stretched out a ginger paw and assessed it critically. "Claw's split," he murmured irritably.

Mati felt he was at risk of losing the story. The ginger tom was easily distracted. "What sort of distances?" he pressed.

Sparrow forgot his claw and resumed with a *pirrup*. "Well, I hear they can travel halfway round the earth! Can you imagine that? Because the earth is mostly water. That's why we don't travel, we cats, the water you know… If it were all land, it would be a different matter entirely. Of course, you like water, don't you, my boy?"

"Not the sea! That's far too big, and salty…" Mati's nose wrinkled. "I couldn't swim in the sea." He had travelled by ship to the dockyard beyond Cressida Lock, all those moons ago. He hadn't minded life onboard, not really. But the endless expanse of water had scared him and he had preferred to remain below deck.

"Well, the tuna did. And he had swum so far that he was lost, but he knew he had to get to his friends soon, because the water in the ocean was too cold for him, and if he stayed there, that would be the end of him!"

"So did he swim home?" asked Mati.

"Well no, he couldn't, he didn't know how, or I should say, he didn't know where! He was well and truly in trouble. And just when he thought it couldn't get any worse, the fishing boats arrived!"

"Oh no! So what happened then?" gasped Mati obligingly, urging Sparrow on.

28

"It was quite a catastrophe!" declared Sparrow. His good eye widened dramatically while his squinty eye seemed to narrow. "They threw the tuna into a cramped tank onboard and set sail. He was in there with all these other fishes that he didn't know, a curious squid, I think it was and yes, some crabs and other crustaceans too of dubious merit and, you can imagine, they didn't get on."

Mati found it hard to imagine fish bickering, but he nodded.

"They kept them in the tank so that they could kill them fresh when they got them to shore. The poor tuna was becoming claustrophobic, for his kind cannot stand confined spaces, you know. They were steaming along the ocean when disaster struck — there was a ghastly storm! The ship was carried miles from land, far away towards the warmer waters. Most of the hinds didn't make it — they can swim, you know, but not awfully well, it really isn't their thing."

Mati thought this was probably true. He couldn't imagine humans swimming easily, or for long distances. They were so ... well, *vertical*.

Sparrow went on. "It was a dreadful business! The tank with the fishes cracked and was leaking something terrible, and the fishes feared they would suffocate for want of water!"

Mati's eyes widened. "They breathe water?"

"Oh yes," said Sparrow authoritatively. "Air kills them,

29

you know – that's why they're fishes. My uncle Roosty had a very curious adventure with a carp once. A carp ... or was it an eel?" Sparrow grew silent, lost in thought.

Mati wanted to hear what had happened to the tuna, so he quickly put in, "But what about the ship, Mr Sparrow, what about the tank? Did all the fishes suffocate?" Sparrow blinked at Mati, disturbed from his memories. "Oh yes, the tank! The tuna!" His eyes sparkled and he took a deep breath before resuming. "They panicked desperately when the water started draining from the tank. Somehow, the tuna managed to wriggle himself free. Breathlessly, he dragged himself across the boards of the ship and threw himself over the deck, down into the ocean. And what do you think happened then?"

Mati shook his head.

"Well, the water that greeted the tuna was warm! And when he looked around, he saw that the ocean had shrunk into a little sea, and that everything looked familiar!"

"He had found his way home!" exclaimed Mati.

"Yes!" agreed Sparrow. "He had made it back, quite by chance! Isn't that remarkable? And all the other tuna from his school came to meet him, and he was happy once more! He was a tuna in a wonderfully warm sea, surrounded by friends and family, and at last he knew he belonged."

Mati opened his eyes. Sparrow was stretched across the far side of the chamber, breathing deeply. His mouth was open, his tongue lolling slightly against the bedding.

A dim light filtered through the open door of the chamber from the overhead grille. Twilight. Mati settled back in the warm chamber and closed his eyes. He waited for sleep to reclaim him. A breeze drifted through the catacombs, nudging the door to-and-fro. Heat rose from the base of his paws. Fiåney was calling. His whiskers trembled, then relaxed. His head felt light, his body weightless. Floating into the dream-wake, the air became a rich, indigo blue. He sensed three passages unfurling before him, tugging him at once in different directions. He started towards the middle passage with fluid steps, as though in slow motion. Dimly, at the end, he saw a sandy hilltop with a small mound of rocks. Beyond it the sky was crimson. Mati started to approach the hilltop through the dream-wake. He paused. From the passage to his left, a voice called his name – the beautiful, sonorous voice of a queen. Mati gasped in surprise and turned his face towards the passage, meaning to approach it, to find the mistress of the voice. Just then he heard another sound emerge from the passage to his right – the long, desperate mewls of cats in pain.

Mati's eyes snapped open and he stood up abruptly, back in the waking world. No. He wouldn't enter those limitless corridors. He did not wish to know what waited along them. He wanted to live now, in the moment – to forget about the past, the battle between the Tygrine and the Sa. What could he understand about these ancient tribes? He was a Cressida Cat, he had a home and a new family.

Mithos was dead. Nothing could hurt him here, in the physical realm. But even as Mati thought this, his ears flicked back. Doubt lingered. What if the danger he had sensed was real? Shouldn't he tell someone? Shouldn't he *do* something?

He padded through the catacombs to the exit by the cherry trees. The stalls were locked, the market-place quiet. The last few humans carried their goods towards the road at the verge of Cressida Lock, packing them into vans. The moon was rising, almost full, ashen and low.

Mati sensed Pangur before he laid eyes on him. The powerful musk of the Chief of the Cressida Cats wafted around him on the evening breeze. And there he was, striding confidently across the cobbles, his tail swishing behind him.

Tell him! ordered a voice in Mati's head. Tell Pangur what you know!

The wind rose over the cherry trees. What do I know? thought Mati. Nothing. There is nothing to tell.

He watched as Pangur made towards his favourite stall, near to the towering elm. Warmth rose from Mati's paws. Voices seemed to stir on the air. He glanced at the quavering leaves of the cherry trees. *Danger*, they murmured, *Escape!* Mati struggled to push the sounds away, to conquer the warmth that ebbed beneath his paws. He thought of returning to Sparrow's comfortable chamber, of sleeping for several hours before stalking the park with Domino. He yearned for a quiet life. If danger was coming, what could he do to prevent it? He didn't want to think about trouble;

about battles, and hardship, sadness and loss. He wanted to be normal, like any other cat. But when he shut his eyes, he saw the murderous Suzerain crossing the desert like black flames. He heard mewls of despair above the snap and hiss of a furious blaze.

Mati opened his eyes. The images had vanished but something bitter lingered on the breeze, like smoke from a distant fire. He wasn't like the others. He knew that. He was the last descendant of the Abyssinia Tygrine, a cat of exceptional instincts. He held in his power the spirit of every cat on earth. He did not understand how this could be, or what it meant.

"You have a gift, and all gifts come with responsibilities." That is what Etheleldra the shalian had told him. What else had she said? "It disquiets the spirits that such gifts should be neglected. This is your destiny."

Before he could talk himself out of it, Mati felt his paws hurrying over the tarmac towards the towering elm.

Sitting upright on his stall, Pangur watched as Mati told him of his fears. "I didn't know what to do," said the catling. "They're just images from the dream-wake. I don't know if they mean anything. But I have a bad feeling... Like I had before the flood, and before Mithos arrived." Mati licked his lips. Even now, long after he had defeated the Suzerain's assassin, the thought of Mithos filled him with fear.

The chief narrowed his eyes. His tail flicked and black

33

coat shimmered in the moonlight. "What would you have us do?"

Mati knew the answer to this – had secretly known for days. He cleared his throat and lowered his face. "We should leave Cressida Lock." He spoke this almost in a whisper.

Pangur frowned. "Did you say leave the Territory? But this is our home."

Mati glanced up. "I could leave. Now, alone." His ears flattened. "It's me that the Suzerain wants. I am the … I am the Tygrine cat." Mati paused. The words still sounded strange. "Maybe you would all be safer if I just went," he finished in a small voice.

Pangur sat in silent thought for a moment, studying the catling. His ears were pointed forward and he seemed relaxed. Only the twitchy beats of his tail betrayed his worries. At length, he shook his head. "We won't leave you to confront your enemies alone. We are a kin – we stand together in the face of danger. If your senses tell you that we should leave Cressida Lock then we must go, and soon. Call the cats to meet here at once. We will decide a plan tonight."

News of the meeting spread quickly and cats gathered on the deserted stalls at the borders of the Territory beside the great elm.

"It's not a full moon until tomorrow," whined Fink, the Siamese cat. "Not a normal meeting, then."

34

"No indeed," agreed Arabella, the Persian, cocking her pretty white head. "I wonder what's going on."

Mati arrived at Pangur's stall. "Mr Pangur, sir, is everyone here?" he asked the chief.

Pangur surveyed the growing crowd. "Most, it would seem. We should begin."

Mati nodded. Then he looked around. "Sparrow! Mr Sparrow isn't here – he must still be resting – I'll get him."

"Quickly!" said Pangur. The surrounding cats were miaowing loudly, curious and impatient. He would have to start the meeting soon.

Mati wove through stalls and hurried towards the catacombs, scrambling into Sparrow's chamber. The ginger tom wasn't there. He ran back across the market-place, reaching Pangur's stall with a breathless shrug.

"I can't wait any longer," said Pangur quietly. "Hop up there so others can see you."

Reluctantly, Mati sprang onto the lower stall next to the chief's.

Pangur addressed the kin. "Silence! I realize that tonight is not a full moon – that I have called upon your time unusually. I will get straight to the point. The Cressida Cats meet tonight because I have learned of great danger at Cressida Lock." The assembled cats gasped. Pangur continued. "As you know, Mati isn't like us. He isn't just a feral. He is *Pirrup*: the Courageous and Sagacious King Mati, Lord of the Tygrine Cats." He said this awkwardly, still not

35

really sure how to address the russet catling. The chief had never been keen on the curious naming formalities of the Cressida Cats and given the Tygrine in their midst, the rituals seemed emptier than ever. They came from a time when the ferals lived in isolation, in the small world of the market-place where hierarchy and order were needed to ensure that everyone got along. The previous chief had loved such accolades, acting like a king of his dominion. Pangur was a young cat, indifferent to tradition. The ferals could call him what they liked – as long as they showed him respect. And what did tradition matter if the kin's isolation was about to end? If the Cressida Cats no longer lived at Cressida Lock? If a catling from the ancient tribes walked in their midst?

Pangur cleared his throat. "Mati's senses are not like others. He can commune with spirits – spirits from Fiåney."

This was news to no one at Cressida Lock. Still, the cats mewed and whispered as though in surprise. Several looked at Mati, whose ears were pressed flat against his head as his tail clung to his flank. He hated the attention.

"Silence!" Pangur snapped, more forcefully, and the crowd hushed. "Mati has heard warnings from the dream-wake. We are no longer safe here. We must leave the market-place."

"Leave?" gasped Trillion, Domino's mother. Remembering that they were in a formal meeting, despite the absence of a full moon, Trillion quickly added their leader's traditional address: *"Pirrup*: the Courageous Chief Pangur, Lord of the Realm, but where would we go?"

"*Pirrup*: the Courageous Chief Pangur, Lord of the Realm, begging your pardon but I have something to say," piped up Domino, sitting by her side.

Pangur's tail swished impatiently. "Go on, kit. Not that you should be here, not until you are grown — catlings are not supposed to attend full-moon meetings, you know that." He glanced at the silver tabbies, Binjax and Ria, who were sitting nearby with their parents, Kroof and Sinestra. Ria lowered her face with a furtive look but Binjax stared back defiantly.

"But it's not a full moon," observed Domino, then faltered, worried that he'd been insolent to the chief.

"You needn't be clever with me," hissed Pangur. "I will let you stay and say your piece, not for the status of the moon but because your friend Mati is an essential part of this meeting, and because the decisions made tonight will affect catlings as much as everyone else." His eyes darted again to Binjax and lingered as he added, "But catlings should remember their place."

"Th-th-thank you, Mr Pangur, sir," Domino stuttered. "I just wanted to say that if Mati says we've *got* to leave, well, we've just got to! It doesn't matter where."

"You'd follow Mati over a cliff if he asked you," Trillion reproved.

"What if I did? He wouldn't ask unless there was a rea-son!" returned Domino stubbornly.

Sinesta stared at the black-and-white. "This is our

Territory, our home. We cannot just leave it! Cressida Cats have lived by the lock since the days of the Great Founders, *Pirrup*: the Courageous Ladies Wilhelmina and Moullier, Consorts of Freedom."

Cats pirruped respectfully at the mention of the kin's foremothers.

Binjax growled in agreement. "I was born at Cressida Lock, and I will die here!" he declared, to a chorus of yowls. "What is this 'danger' anyway?" he added quietly to his sister, Ria. "What is a 'king' without subjects? I don't see anything so special about Mati anyway."

Mati stole a quick look in the silver tabby's direction, having heard what he said. Binjax had been hostile from the outset. And yet he had protected Mati, putting his own life at risk when the Suzerain's assassin had arrived at Cressida Lock. Mati still felt stunned by this gesture, confused that Binjax continued to refuse his friendship, after everything that had happened.

"The Tygrine has made a mistake," agreed Fink. "He cannot possibly expect us to abandon the catacombs and wander off into nowhere. We are not a pack of wild dogs. We have territory. We have a purpose!"

"Hear, hear!" agreed Arabella, and others put in words of agreement.

"Listen before you judge!" warned Pangur, green eyes glaring. "Your memories are short. Do you not recall Mithos, the cat only Mati could defeat? Who here has forgotten

38

the horror felt by all on that night, when Mati faded into shadow? He may not wish to lead us, but this cat is special. If he senses danger, ours is not to question. Mati knows what he feels, and we ignore him at our peril."

Some of the cats quietened at this speech, considering Pangur's words. Others were more suspicious.

"We cannot be expected to leave without understanding why," said Torko, previously one of the Kanks. "With all respect to Mati, this is asking too much."

"How will we live out there, outside Cressida Lock?" put in Ria, Binjax's sister. She peered nervously towards the verges of the market-place where the road hummed with cars. "What would we eat?"

"What exactly has Mati seen?" pressed her mother, Sinestra. "What has he seen in the dream-wake?"

Fink leaned over and whispered in Arabella's ear. "He's only a catling, barely more than a kit. Perhaps he thinks this is some sort of joke?"

"He's playing with us," she agreed.

Mati crouched down, lowering his face. The meeting wasn't going well. Was he really foolish enough to believe that the cats would agree to leave their home, just like that? Without a reason, plan or destination? His old enemy Binjax had asked what the danger was – and this was surely understandable? The cats deserved an explanation. But Mati couldn't give them one – he couldn't put this feeling into words. He glanced overhead, between the leaves of the mighty elm. Beyond them the world was dark, starless and still. The sky around Mati felt heavy, as though before a storm. He caught a wisp of acrid smoke and crinkled his nose. To his watchful senses, the night was crackling with omens. Even the ashen moon seemed to throb in deathly warning. He felt with growing certainty that a great darkness was coming to Cressida Lock – that this was only the beginning.

As the cats talked across each other, Sinestra's words circled Mati's mind: "What has he seen in the dream-wake?" He closed his eyes. In an instant he was back in the desert, at the scene of an ancient battle. His fur bristled instinctively and his heart started racing. He saw the Suzerain advancing and opened his mouth to speak. No words came, only silent entreaties that hung on the arid air.

Most of the ferals were arguing over Pangur, ignoring Mati, who sat alone on the lower stall. But Trillion was watching him keenly. She frowned. Suddenly, she forgot she was a Cressida Cat, eager to stay in the Territory. The vulnerability in the small russet catling awakened her tenderness. She glanced at her own son, Domino. "Mati's scared," she said quietly.

Behind the boarded-up church, Sparrow cupped his orange paw and reached into a disused pipe. There was an object inside it, less than a tail-length away – it smelled tasty. Sparrow sniffed appreciatively and tried again, stretching his paw deeper. His stubby claws brushed against cardboard. Concentrating, he tried again. With a swipe, two claws hooked onto the small box. Sparrow eased it out from within the pipe and it plopped on the tarmac in front of him.

He inspected the box. The writing meant nothing to him. Neither did the image of a rat in a circle, with a red diagonal line striking through it – this was just window dressing to the fine-smelling food within. Pressing his paw on the box to keep it still, Sparrow was able to squeeze his ginger muzzle inside. He reached out his tongue and began lapping at the dried meat.

He squinted, his eyes stinging. There was something bitter about the food – something unpleasant. Sparrow yanked his muzzle out of the box. He had heard a commotion at the other end of the market-place, the sound of yowling carried on the evening breeze. Confused, he looked into the sky. The waxing moon was large but a hazy darkness fringed one side – it would not be full for a day or two. The kin's regular meetings were usually held on a full moon. Could one be in session, nonetheless? Had someone told him about it? Should he be there? Sparrow had a habit of forgetting such things.

He abandoned the box with its tangy meat, starting around the boarded-up church and across the cobbled market-place. After a moment, he stopped for breath. "Don't feel like me ... don't feel me at all," he murmured.

Sparrow tried to wash himself but his paws trembled,

41

suddenly uncoordinated; the pads were damp. He started again towards the elm on wobbling legs. "It will pass..." he assured himself. His stomach clenched. A searing pain shot through his chest.

With a tiny mewl, his face hit the ground.

The Eye of the Moon

Far away, in the Nile Delta, the city of Zagazig slept. The occasional car rattled along its dusty streets and music floated on the warm air from a radio by an open window. It was as close to silence as the city ever reached; the nearest it came to perfect peace.

To a human eye, there was little of interest to be seen that night, and nothing at all to be feared. But a cat's eye sees deeper through the darkness. A gibbous moon hung over the skyline, hunched like a predator waiting to pounce.

The secret palace in the heart of the city was crackling with activity: beyond layers of crumbling brickwork, sentinels marched up and down the gloomy passages, muscular cats with long legs and sharp fangs. Within the inner chamber, high priests circled the Suzerain, who sat silent in the half-light. Head lowered, he followed their incantations:

Harakar, Harakar
Those who sleep
Deep within the silent land
Those who wander endlessly
Those whose eyes no longer see

Limping on ancient, brittle bones, Ipanel struggled towards the Suzerain's chamber. He had heard of the master's devastating plan. He had vowed to stop it – whatever the cost. Ipanel was the court's oldest shalian, a mystic who had survived numerous plots, feuds and skirmishes in his years at the palace. He had tutored the Suzerain from kittenhood, had taught him the ways of Fiåney before the great leader had the faintest inklings of his own power. Fiåney was the land of spirits and the feline second self – not the world of dreams but the mysterious maze that wove between them and the waking world. Ipanel knew better than most that only exceptional cats could enter Fiåney at will. Some became experts at moving between the realms, growing ever more powerful with the force of the dream-wake, and this was true of the Suzerain. The Cat Lord outshone his tutor, even as a catling, and now, Ipanel realized, it was difficult to estimate the Suzerain's capabilities; hard to imagine how far he would go in his quest to avenge the legacy of Sa.

Ipanel had been a formidable teacher – fierce and exacting. Even as an old cat, there were few who would tangle with him. He was feared and respected throughout the court; more powerful, even, than the Commander in Chief of the Army of the Sa Mau. The Suzerain would have to listen to him.

"Halt!" ordered a sentinel as the shalian approached the inner chamber.

"It is I, fool!" spat Ipanel.

"Apologies, Wise One – but the Master said that none were to enter."

The old cat limped past the sentinel, who dared not stop him. "He did not mean me!" hissed the shalian as he shuffled beneath the statue of the one-eyed cobra, into the inner chamber.

The high priests were chanting:

Those who know the Tygrine's secret
Those who feel the Sa Mau's hate

Ipanel pushed past the circling priests. "O Master, I must speak to you presently!" he cried, breathless, dipping his head. No time for polite introductions – he had to stop this insanity, before it was too late.

At once, the chanting ceased. The high priests froze in their tracks and gazed at the shalian.

The Suzerain sat quite still. Without turning, he spoke. "Ipanel, my old tutor."

"Master, forgive my impudence, but I urge you not

to open that gate! What you wish for defies the laws of nature. We shall conquer the Tygrine, we shall take him with armies, with trackers and slayers. But not like this..." The shalian's heart fluttered against his aged ribs. Fiâney still called to him, murmured his name as it always did. Yet beyond the voice of the dream-wake, another reached his ears. He felt a coldness press closer. It was death, the shalian knew. How long had it had been hovering over his shoulder, waiting to claim him?

"You will not stop me," growled the Suzerain. "Do you consider that your many moons of tutelage protect you – that your services to Sa defend you? You should know better. Your lessons trained me to hate the Tygrine above all others. Your service taught me to despise mercy as weakness."

"I do not counsel forgiveness, My Lord," the shalian assured. "Old wounds shall never be healed – that is what we have always said; that is what we continue to believe." He gasped a shallow breath. His energy was failing him. Urgently, he pressed on. "Yet, O Master, this is not the way."

"I know that the timing is less than ideal. I would have waited for the moon to brim and fill in earnest, were it not for such distractions as you and others throw at my court. Of course the moon *should* be full, I realize that. To release the Three before a full moon is to endanger their passage – they may not emerge as once they were."

"They could be deformed, Sire. They could be depraved!"

"I am aware of the risks, but there is no time to waste for release of the hunters. The gate *will* open. The Tygrine's powers grow, even though he cannot know it – soon he may be harder to defeat. Great Spirit Alia agrees. Who are you to compel me to stop? You are but a mystic: not royalty; not even a lower-order spirit."

"Be it now or beneath a full moon, it is nature that compels you, not I," said the shalian. "Nature forbids what you seek. The world of the spirits and that of blood are separate domains. And now you summon the orb, the omens, to this eternal war. No good can result from the moon at arms…"

The Suzerain growled – a chilling sound that curdled the blood. "The moon is a natural ally to the Empire of Sa. It is our friend, the eye of the night. When full, this eye will guide the Three, guide them to where the Tygrine hides. The moon will find him, and so shall I." Slowly, the Suzerain began to turn. The high priests backed towards the walls of the chamber. Their fear rose in wafts, overpowering the incense that hung in the air.

The Cat Lord spoke. "You travel to the dream-wake, Ipanel, as do I. And many times, you return. No harm comes to you on these journeys – no harm befalls the world of cats, the realm of the first self."

"That is different, My Lord. We are of blood. We are still of blood…"

The Suzerain turned his eyes on his shalian. The old cat

staggered. Darkness washed over him. He felt the fragile life draining from his body. "You light a fire that will be impossible to extinguish," Ipanel gasped. "Nature shall have its revenge. The kingdom of Sa will be damned!"

The Suzerain looked away. "Continue," he uttered, his voice steely, addressing the priests, who renewed their chants.

Those who know the Tygrine's secret
Those who feel the Sa Mau's hate
We bid entry to our kingdom
No more centuries to wait...

The chamber flashed white but the nervous priests kept chanting:

We shall guide you out of chaos!
We shall lead you to the gate!

A high-pitched crackle vibrated through the chamber. Deep within Fiåney, dark matter formed as sweeping dust to rise in plumes of smoke. Palls of grey spun into reaching cobwebs, crystallizing, taking shape as distorted feline bodies – echoes of cats that had walked the earth before many ages of the moon.

The twisted forms of three spirits broke free of the colourless halls where they had wandered for centuries. Warped with time and bitterness, they melded together and broke apart, like the waves of a dark ocean, settling into a single, disfigured creature. Its instinct told it only to destroy.

The high priests cowered against the walls of the chamber, horrified.

But the Suzerain was jubilant. "Death to the Tygrine traitor!" he hissed, addressing the creature gleefully. "Race to find Mati at Cressida Lock! Find him, kill him, and I will reward you for your service – I will give you that thing which your heart desires: this I swear."

Something passed between the Suzerain and the creature.

It gazed at him with six eyes, and seemed to agree to his terms. "S-w-e-a-r," it rasped. "*S-w-e-a-r.*"

The Cat Lord dipped his head. "I am the Suzerain, high leader of the Sa Mau. We are friends, you have my word. But only if you kill the Tygrine pure-blood – if you rid him from this world. Do not spare the Tygrine cat, whatever his entreaties." He turned his black eyes on Ipanel. "Show no mercy for any who seek to protect him. Death to the Tygrine's friends! Death to enemies of justice!"

Raging, bewildered, the creature pounced upon the shalian.

"Take me, Fiåney," whimpered Ipanel. "Always have I served you…" But the halls of the dream-wake met his cries with silence. Another voice replied. The icy voice he had already heard. The one he most dreaded with every last beat of his heart.

49

"Come, Ipanel..."

"Nature is defeated!" the shalian murmured. "Damn the tribes to eternal war! A curse upon you both! The Tygrine and the Sa are the servants of the Harakar. Let them perish in that terrible realm, and with them every cat on earth!"

They were the last words he spoke.

Silent Strangers

The ferals bickered, uncertain whether to trust their leader and the ruddy brown catling who sat silently on a lower stall. It was Trillion who finally interrupted. "We have no choice but to leave Cressida Lock." She spoke again, more loudly: "We have no choice. If we stay here, it will be the end of us."

One by one, the ferals fell silent.

"Why do you say that?" ventured Sinestra.

Trillion nodded at Mati. "The catling is terrified. He has seen danger. It is etched in his face."

They turned to stare at Mati. He licked his lips. He knew that he should speak, that he must try to persuade them. "It's true," he said in a small voice. "I am scared. I have seen things." He looked up at Pangur, who urged him with a blink to continue. Above the chief, Mati caught sight of the moon, which drifted low and pale. He swallowed and went on. "I don't want to … to upset anyone. I don't want to cause any trouble. I would rather stay here too."

"But what *has* he seen?" pressed Binjax to a chorus of miaows.

Mati frowned at Binjax. He can't bring himself to address me, he thought. Muscles tensing, Mati shut his eyes. For a few seconds, there was nothing. Then he heard it, the rumble and whirr of that terrifying land, the crackle and spit of flames. His eyes flicked open. "Cats of the Sa Mau," he said. "Cats of war. Shadows crossing Cressida Lock. Death…" He trembled and the words snagged in his throat. The wind had changed, drifting west, and with it he had caught a sound. His chest contracted, a knot formed in his throat.

Pangur and the others stared in surprise as Mati leapt off the stall and hurried across the market-place. A moment later they heard a wail that chilled their blood.

Mati was pawing at Sparrow, whimpering, when the others arrived.

"What's happened?" asked Pangur, aghast.

Mati ignored him. "Wake up, Mr Sparrow!" he begged, butting the ginger's face with his nose.

Sparrow moaned. One eye opened a crack. "Bad … food…" he managed. "From a box."

Trillion took a step closer. "If it's something he ate, he needs to chew on grass." All cats knew that the way to get

52

rid of a stomach ache was to swallow grass and bring on sickness.

"He's in no state for that," said Fink, but already Mati was running to the park at the verge of the market-place, tearing off tufts of grass with his teeth, with Domino right behind him. The other ferals exploded into activity, collecting grass while Trillion coaxed Sparrow to eat it. Soon they had a circle of grass surrounding Sparrow — more than any cat could manage. Pangur alone strayed over the cobbles towards the boarded-up church.

Groggily, Sparrow chewed on the grass, which fell from his lips in damp clumps, clods of soil still hanging from stringy ends. He groaned, lightly shaking his head. "No more," he begged.

"Go on!" insisted Trillion. "Just another bite. That's it."

Sparrow gagged, swallowed and started to retch. A moment later he threw up violently as the other cats watched in relief.

Mati's tail shot up and he started to purr.

The ginger cat looked sheepishly at the grass-strewn vomit on the tarmac and the wide-eyed ferals surrounding him. "Just a little tummy bug." He chuckled, and this gave way to a cough. He cleared his throat. "Can't get rid of me that easily!"

Mati went to wash Sparrow's ears. He noticed Pangur some paces away, appearing from behind the boarded-up church. The chief stalked swiftly towards the gathered kin.

His face was grim. "I found the box, the one with the food. It had a peculiar smell." Pangur's jaw stiffened. "I think it was poisoned."

The shocked ferals absorbed this revelation in silence.

The next day, Mati and Domino wandered together to the park, while Sparrow slept off the after-effects of the poison. It would be their last time here among the asters, their last time stretching in beams of sunlight along the thinning grass.

The little harlequin catling batted at a bee. "This bad feeling you have..." he started, not meeting Mati's eye. "What do you think would ... would happen to us? I mean, if we stayed here?"

"Be careful, that thing could sting you," said his russet-coated friend.

"That thing? It's just a fly!"

Mati frowned. "It can sting."

"Really? How do you know that?" Domino had the bee pinned beneath a white paw.

"I think you should let it go."

"No chance!" scoffed Domino. "Do you know how hard it is to catch flies? Reckon I'll eat it," he pronounced, tightening his grip.

Mati blinked. In that instant, he saw Domino screaming with pain, a tiny pod hooked to the pad of his paw, pumping out venom as Mati looked on helplessly. "I'm warning you," snarled Mati. He pictured Domino racing across the park, whimpering, desperate, his paw smarting and swollen. "Let it go!" he spat suddenly.

Domino jumped, taken aback. The bee shot free and looped over their heads before buzzing away. "What's wrong with you?" demanded Domino. "You're losing it! It's just a furry fly!"

Mati's ears twitched. "I thought ... it could sting."

"You didn't have to shout! I've been stung by nettles before. Big deal! I'm not a kit, you know!" Domino stared at Mati in disbelief, tail puffed.

"Sorry," murmured Mati.

The black-and-white softened. "Maybe the thing with Sparrow is getting to you. He'll be OK, Pangur said so."

Mati longed to tell his friend about the images from Fiåney. He wanted to explain that the insect could really hurt him – perhaps it could even kill him. But that would sound absurd. After all, it *was* just some sort of fly, wasn't it?

"Cheer up, fella!" said Domino with a mischievous glint in his eyes. "Come on, let's go and hunt for some grub."

That night, the entire kin gathered by the cherry trees beneath a full moon. Sad green eyes peered from grave faces.

"Amma, I don't want to go," whined a ginger-and-white kitten called Scallion. His sister Pips, a tawny tabby with a white bib, nodded her head in agreement.

"I know, my kits," replied Pritin, their mother, washing Scallion's head. Like Pips she was tabby-and-white, although her markings were more random than her daughter's. "None of us do, but it isn't safe here."

"Because of what happened to Mr Sparrow?"

"Yes, in a way. In a way that we cannot understand."

Pangur walked slowly over the cobbles towards the waiting cats.

"But I was born here," whispered Pips.

"We all were, child," murmured Pritin.

"Pangur wasn't, he walked a great distance to reach the lock, he told us so himself," said Fink, who had sidled up behind them. "No disrespect intended, of course," he added quickly.

"Mati wasn't either," added Arabella, exchanging a meaningful look with her Siamese friend.

Pangur took a step closer, shooting them a warning glance. He hadn't heard their words but he could guess from their lowered tones that they were still questioning his decision to leave.

Standing next to Sparrow a short distance away, Mati lowered his eyes. With his keen hearing, he had caught every word. It was not only Arabella and Fink that gave him cause for concern. He sensed the doubts of other cats, unspoken, hanging in the air. Peering up, he caught sight of the full moon. In the past he had scarcely concerned himself with that distant orb. Tonight, though, a red corona glowed around it, visible to Mati's eyes alone, and a tremor of fear awakened in him.

"Cats of Cressida Lock," said the chief, "in which I include the Kanks who have joined us. The time has come to depart this place. We have a journey ahead of us – the world stands before us. Who here does not crave adventure? Who here is scared of the unknown? We have lived happily at Cressida Lock, but the time has come to leave."

"What if the catling is wrong?" pressed Fink.

Pangur shook his head. "He is the King of the Tygrine cats. I trust him." He glanced at Mati, who blinked back gratefully.

"What does that even mean?" asked Arabella. "What does it mean to be a king without a tribe?" She had heard this point being made by Binjax and, like others, had fallen upon it to question Mati's authority.

"*We* are his tribe," said Domino. Standing behind him, his mother Trillion nodded. Sparrow puffed up his chest and pirruped enthusiastically.

Mati eyed Pangur, wondering if this oath of loyalty would disturb the chief. But if it did, the black tom showed no sign of it. "Come," said Pangur, "it is time to leave." He turned towards the park downstream and strode purposefully away from the cobbled market-place. Reluctantly, the cats started to follow.

Mati levelled with Pangur. "Not that way, Mr Pangur, sir."

The chief hesitated. "You arrived from downstream, all those moons ago. I assumed..."

The Tygrine didn't reply. He stared for a moment towards the park where he had once met Etheleldra. His whiskers inched forward. He could feel a distant shudder through the base of his paws, the vibrations of something hurrying towards them, far away but advancing swiftly. From these movements, Mati could not be sure if it was one creature, or many – the pace seemed strange, uncat-like, despite something feline in the stride – and no smell reached him on the late summer air. It moved almost chaotically, as though ill coordinated, and yet with some mysterious purpose. Mati sensed a nature that could not rest, that would never give up.

Heat rose from the catling's paws. Calling him from the park, from deep inside a hollow tree that no longer existed, the voice of Etheleldra came to him suddenly. "You must escape! They approach!"

Standing next to Mati, Pangur heard nothing of this warning. He had no power to enter Fiåney, to commune with shalians and spirits. But the chief caught the alarm in Mati's golden eyes. "Very well, we shall journey upstream. The road circles there, but I know of a path that runs beneath it, along the river, that the hinds use. Few should bother us at night."

With difficulty, Mati tore his gaze away from the park and the dark world beyond. "Mr Pangur ... sir ... What if I'm wrong?"

Pangur shook his head. "Believe in yourself, Mati." The fierce intensity of his dark features relaxed and his white fangs glinted. "It's an adventure, isn't it? It can't be all bad! Takes me back to my roving days as a young cat."

Mati stared at the chief. He admired the tom's bold, unerring beauty, the force of his confidence, of his faith and his will. In a flash, Mati saw the inquisitive kitten that Pangur once was. Even from a young age, he possessed an air of authory that drew others to him. He lacked Mati's ability to enter the dream-wake, to explore the second self or tangle with the thoughts of other cats. Unlike Mati, he was not weighed down by such burdens. Yet an undefined power of its own radiated from the tom's glossy fur.

With tail raised high, Pangur began to lead his kin upstream.

But as the cats drew away from the cherry trees, a voice rang out.

"I am staying!"

They turned to see Binjax. He sat between the cherry trees, ears forward, straight-backed. "I was born at Cressida Lock and I will die here!"

"Don't be foolish!" snapped Pangur.

"I'm staying," insisted Binjax. "And I am not alone!"

"I'm staying too," said his sister, Ria, in a small voice.

Fink's eyes grew round with delight. "And me!"

The effect of Binjax's announcement was immediate. One after another, Cressida Cats broke from Pangur's kin to join the tabby catling at the cherry trees. The cats were territorial animals with a fierce sense of belonging, a connection to the land. Few, if any, actually wanted to leave the comfort of their homes for the uncertainties beyond the Territory.

"I am old," murmured a skinny queen, as she turned to Binjax. "Sorry, Chief Pangur," she added with a backwards glance. The black tom glared at her and she lowered her gaze.

Mati watched in silence as the kin divided. He had not expected this; had not imagined that they would challenge Pangur's authority. What more could he do to persuade them of the danger? What else could he say?

"Safety in numbers," said Arabella, joining her friend Fink. "We should stick together. If most of the kin want to stay, well…"

Following her, Torko added, "More hazards outside the Territory, isn't that right?"

Pangur stood, perfectly still but for his black tail, which twitched with agitation.

Trillion levelled alongside him. She scolded Binjax and the cats that crowded round him. "Have you heard nothing? It *is* dangerous to stay here. We have to leave – we have no choice. Now even former members of the Kanks turn their backs on the leader who welcomed them in, the brother of Hanratty. Your rebellion is not only disloyal, it is reckless, stupid!"

Stung by these words, Torko – himself a former Kank – paused, turned and rejoined Pangur's group.

"Where do you think you're going!" hissed Binjax. "Coward! Running away. Don't you see it is Mati who's stupid, him and all those who agree with his plan!"

Trillion opened her mouth to respond, but Pangur caught her eye. "Let him stay," he said quietly. "Better he takes his chances here than jeopardizes the journey with his carping and divisiveness."

"Better he stays to die, you mean?" replied Trillion, but her voice was louder than Pangur's and she was overhead by Sinestra, mother to Binjax and Ria, who had been standing a few paces behind.

"My kits, you mustn't stay here!" Sinestra exclaimed. "You heard Pangur. Look what happened to Sparrow! It isn't safe."

"Our leader has spoken," said Kroof, their father. "Come, let's have no more arguments."

Binjax shook his head. "This is my home and I won't leave it. Not for Pangur. Not for the Tygrine. Not for *anyone*." A large group of cats now surrounded him, watching this exchange. Only a handful remained with the chief: Mati, Domino, Trillion, Sparrow, Torko the Kank and Pritin with her kittens. Sinestra had moved a few paces towards her son, with Kroof by her side.

"Not even for me?" murmured Sinestra.

"Enough!" snapped the chief, tail beating the air impatiently. He narrowed his eyes. His face did not register any sense of betrayal. Even his anger was cool. "I will not stop you, Binjax. I won't stop any of you." He glared at the ferals

61

who had retreated to the cherry trees. "Live here, with the catling. Die here if you wish. Those who care to, follow me now – we shall have no further discussion on the matter."

Pangur strode away, followed by the small number of cats who still treated him as their leader.

Mati dropped back. Nervously, he approached the silver tabbies and their parents. The remaining ferals stood nearby, glancing at each other. Some hadn't really expected Pangur to leave without them.

"Please," urged Mati. "It is dangerous here. I can feel them … *it* … coming closer. You should leave with us."

Ria glanced uncertainly from Mati to Binjax.

"Rubbish!" Binjax declared. "There is nothing to fear here. This is Cressida Lock!"

Pangur and his small band of ferals were arriving at the borders of the market-place and its fringe of terraced houses. From the other direction, beyond the park, the curious vibrations reached Mati on the wind. He shuddered. "It will be here soon … I don't know how much time we have – we need to leave now. I hope you come too. All of you…" He tore away from them and started after the kin.

"I think we should go with the others," said Ria. "What if he's right? Remember Mithos?"

"Your sister is right. Come with us," said Sinestra.

Binjax looked at his mother. "You could always stay here, Amma." He said it matter-of-factly, as though he didn't care whether she stayed or went.

"The others are leaving," said Kroof. "We don't want to lose them." He began to walk away.

Sinestra followed. She paused, turned back, resting her gaze on her son. "Binjax, I cannot make you come. You are a young tom now, free to roam the land, to do as you please. I am your amma, and I wish you to be near me, at least through the winter. Perhaps in the spring you can break away... But if you choose to stay, I will not prevent you." She turned to her daughter. "Ria, you will of course come. You are younger than your brother, not ready to face the world alone. You cannot remain here." She followed Kroof towards the terraces at the border of the market-place. She walked with a stoop, her ears flat. But she did not turn again.

The ferals who had chosen to stay at Binjax's side looked increasingly uncertain, shifting from paw to paw or washing themselves fretfully.

"I'm not going anywhere!" said Binjax. "None of us are." He threw a warning look at any who dared meet his gaze.

"I'm sorry..." Ria broke from them and rushed after the disappearing kin, her tail skimming the tarmac. This was too much for Arabella, who hastened after the silver tabby.

"Arabella?" called Fink in surprise.

"Back to the catacombs, all of you!" snapped Binjax. The cats stared at him, ears flicking back. Pangur and the others could no longer be seen along the row of terraces. Binjax spoke again, his voice gentler but still defiant. "Go back to the catacombs, don't worry about them – let them run away like scared kits. They'll return soon enough. They'll spend a night or two outside the Territory and come home. We know better. There is nothing to fear at Cressida Lock."

Binjax's words helped to settle the nervous ferals. Yet a sense of disquiet remained, even as several of the cats retreated to the catacombs. It lingered beneath the glowing moon.

Binjax sat beneath the cherry trees, long after the last of Pangur's band had disappeared from view. Already, he missed the chatter of his sister, her chirps, *pirrups* and miaows. He was not used to being apart from her and the silence unnerved him. He thought several times of hurrying after her – of tracking Pangur's scent on the night air.

But Binjax was proud. "They'd tease me," he said. "They'd mock me after so many of the kin stayed behind. I am their leader now, the youngest leader the kin has ever known." Some distance away by the old locked stalls, several of the cats who had remained were whispering among themselves. Binjax frowned. "Talking about me, no doubt. Questioning their decision to stay, doubting my leadership. I'll show them. I'll be a great chief – the best of all." Still, he wished that Ria would return. He hadn't expected her to leave him. He tried to forget about his mother – the idea of losing her was too painful. Of course, it was Mati's fault. Prophesies of doom. Murmurings from the dream-wake. "Tygrine mumbo-jumbo," Binjax grumbled. He started to wash himself.

A wind rose on the market-place as he licked his striped paw. The leaves of the cherry trees rustled above him. He lifted his head. He could just make out someone emerging from the park, shifting beyond the stalls. Binjax narrowed his eyes. The body moved strangely, unnaturally, as though leaping, then stooping. An injured cat, perhaps? A cat with a broken leg... Binjax sniffed the air but could sense nothing of the creature's identity. He glanced over his shoulder, into the darkness of the surrounding riverbank. When he looked back towards the park he suddenly saw three cats, not one, and they were almost at the cobbled market-place. How had they reached it already? No cat would move so swiftly. No earthly creature could...

The ferals near the locked stalls had risen to their paws and were watching with fur raised. They realized immediately that something was wrong; that the limping, distorted creature crossing the market-place was the one that Mati had warned them of – that all too quickly, the danger had arrived. That like Mithos, they could never hope to defeat this juddering stranger.

"It's here!" gasped Fink. *"It's here!"* Panic rippled across Cressida Lock. Ferals burst out of catacombs and started fleeing downstream, away from Binjax and the cherry trees. Not one remained.

Binjax felt the hairs rise on his neck. His back arched instinctively, a growl caught in his throat. The cats approaching him were jerking, twisting. But were they cats?

Their bodies were dark, their movements unreal. Their eyes were amber, almost translucent.

He thought of running, of following Fink and the others downstream, but the shadowy stranger blocked his way. He shot a glance towards the terraces that lined the verge of the market-place, wondering how far Pangur and his company had already travelled. He started to turn but a sound made him freeze in his tracks. A terrible "hisssssssss", so close to his ears that he felt the fur around them flutter, as if someone had pressed against them, had whispered directly into them. Still, there was no odour, nothing cat-like. Nothing that made sense.

"Hissssss," he heard again, this time inside him, throbbing within his ears, drumming against his skull. Above it rose a sound like the crackle and spit of fire. For a desperate moment Binjax thought of the cats he had known: of Ria; of Kroof; of his mother and the life he had lived at Cressida Lock. Of the life he had loved. "The Tygrine was right!" he cried out.

The hiss within his mind formed a broken word. *"Wh-e-re?"*

Mati was with Ria and his parents. "No," he growled. "I won't betray them."

"Wh-e-re? Wh-e-re?"

He heard this even as he fell to the ground, sea-green eyes closing for ever.

The market-place was deserted. The stalls were locked

and abandoned and, beneath the cobbles, the catacombs were vacant. Under the bowing branches of the cherry trees, a silver tabby lay motionless. Three shadows drifted over him, melding into a quivering mass and blurring against the riverbank. Their long, rasping "hissssss" gave way to silence.

The Restless River

The underpass below the road had taken Pangur and his company to the far side of the river. Thereafter, they followed the bank as it wound its way upstream. For the most part the walkways were wide enough for humans to follow. The grassy verges were littered with signs of their visits – empty beer cans, chocolate wrappers and the lingering stench of dogs. The cats trod warily through these paths, their noses twitching at the unsavoury odours.

Leading the way, Pangur turned to Mati. "Is there anywhere, I wonder, that hinds have not sullied?"

Mati shrugged. It seemed unlikely. Evidence of human expansion, of their ceaseless intervention, was there for all to see: buildings; streetlamps; roads; traffic. Yet a voice in him said: "Yes – there is a land where cats alone gather upon a hilltop. Our kind walked there long before the age of hinds. Further south, reeds bow to a river of life, where water has flowed since the dawn of time." Mati did not know where this thought came from, and so he said nothing. He peered overhead, searching for the moon, but it hid, concealed, in a cloudy sky.

Next to Mati ambled Sparrow, and behind them Trillion and Domino. The cats progressed, light-pawed, beneath weeping willows that brushed the water with leafy fingertips. The city unravelled before them. Mati's eyes were slits, his whiskers keenly edging forward, his ears flicking this way and that. He heard traffic, music and the distant hoot of an owl. Peering out of a high nest in the branches of a maple tree, bleary-eyed squirrels blinked down at the passing cats, awoken from their slumber. Rats eyed them from tall grass, baring their yellow teeth.

Pips and Scallion, Pritin's kittens, chatted excitedly between themselves. Their pace was erratic. Sometimes they would stop to exchange a word about an unknown scent, or the sound of traffic on a distant road. Then they raced to catch up with the rest of the kin. They treated the expedition as an escapade that took them away from their sheltered lives at Cressida Lock. The older cats were more thoughtful. Each step of the way presented new smells; a threat of dogs; of wandering strays; of territorial toms. They worried about unguessed perils: the unexplained dangers that lurked behind them, and those that waited before them, stalking the concrete contours of the city at night.

* * *

For hours the cats journeyed along the snaking riverbank that ran through the city. Occasionally, the verge grew so narrow that they had to walk in single file, with Pritin nudging her kittens just ahead of her. Such proximity to the swirling waters made the cats uneasy, but after all they were ferals of the lock, and the river gave them some comfort – a constant reminder of home.

Whimpers and mews came from the kittens, and older cats like Torko and Sparrow grew weary. Pangur sidled up to Mati. "Soon we must rest," he told him.

The Tygrine blinked his golden eyes. Bats dived overhead, hunting insects that hovered above the surface of the river. Summer was waning. A sharper breeze carried across the water from downstream, lifting Mati's fur. The wind was on his side, sending him clues – it came from Cressida Lock, and beyond. With it, Mati sensed the murmurings of the shadowy creature that stalked the night. He still felt it, lost, for now, but searching. "Soon," he agreed. "But not yet."

"We venture south," said the chief. He had never questioned Mati's directions and he did not do so now – though his observation hung in the air.

"South," echoed Mati. He thought about this a moment. He had not considered their route. He only felt that it was sensible to follow the river away from Cressida Lock. No, not *sensible* exactly – instinctively, it felt right. "Closer," said

Etheleldra's voice in Mati's ear. "Come closer. Still too far. Hurry…" The voice faded.

Pangur nodded and said no more.

Pips skipped along beside her mother, a miniature version of the tabby-and-white queen. "Amma," she said, "are we home?"

"Not yet," said Pritin, prodding the kitten forward with her nose.

Next to them scampered Scallion. "What's that, Amma?" He indicated the row of leaning bicycles under a shelter. Most of them looked battered and broken, perhaps abandoned.

"Hinds use them to move around."

"But hinds have legs… Why can't they use their legs?"

"Only two legs, though," Pips pointed out.

"That's true," her brother agreed, glancing suspiciously at the bicycles. "Will our new home be as good as Cressida Lock?" he added.

"We shall see," crooned his mother.

Mati frowned. *Home.* The word reminded him of his old friend Jess and his tail coiled miserably around his flank. She had left him to return to her old man. Just as his mother had left him to enter the halls of the spirits. *They all leave, in the end.*

In front of him, Pangur came to a stop. "The kin must rest. We could steal a few hours under the shelter here. We should also think about food… After a short sleep, I will go out with the stronger hunters to see what we can find."

The branches of the willows stooped and swayed on the breeze. A robin perched on the iron ridge of a streetlamp. Disoriented by the light, he called to his mate, foregoing sleep for the dangers of the night. One by one the cats fell silent as they passed the lonely robin.

The first specks of daylight hung over the gloomy river, which spread ahead of them uncertainly. The moon had set beyond the grey outline of the sleeping city. Mati no longer sensed the creature approaching on the breeze. He thought about Cressida Lock: the pretty cherry trees, the noisy market and the colourful park. In his heart, he felt that it no longer existed as he now remembered it – not as it once had – even though he and the others in Pangur's company had left it only hours earlier. A wave of sadness crashed over him. It was as though the road behind them was vanishing with each step forward.

Despite that, he would have liked to keep going, just a little longer. But already his legs throbbed with fatigue and his eyes felt heavy. How would the kittens be feeling, or the old cats like Sparrow? Reluctantly, he nodded at Pangur. For now, they would sleep – but not too long, and not too deep.

Mistress of Shadows

In the city of Zagazig, many leagues away from Pangur's company and the river they followed upstream, another waterway pressed against crumbling banks. Where mudflats and tall grasses once lined the fringes of this eastern river, now it lay confined, walled within concrete. Nearby, shabby tower blocks stretched into the distance.

Sitting at the riverbank, a young queen reached out a speckled paw and began to wash herself. The morning was fresh, cast in a mellow light. For a moment, the queen caught her reflection on the dappled water; her long, pointed ears; her tall, regal frame. Her black-rimmed eyes had always marked her out from other cats, as one was golden, the other green. She lowered her paw and peered into the sky. Clouds scudded overhead, caught on high currents. A fresh breeze played on her velvety face but a curious heat rose from her paws; her fur prickled along her back. Ears flat, she turned towards the rising expanses of Zagazig – the modern city built on the ruins of an ancient kingdom. She padded along its grimy streets. Tradesmen whizzed past her on bikes and mopeds, whipping up shrouds of dust. The queen blinked against it, edging closer to the walls along narrow pavements. Her paws still coursed with heat, as though the ground beneath them was baking, but she knew it to be cool in the morning air. Her heart started thumping as she hurried through the side streets. When she reached a set of steep steps that led to the heart of the city, the queen began to run.

The Suzerain felt the young cat's presence, even before she had passed below the sign of the red paw of the Sa Mau – the only external marking to his palace beyond the ventilator shaft. He dismissed the high priests and ordered the sentinels to let the queen pass. He would speak to her alone.

In moments she stepped inside, head lowered. She crouched at the Suzerain's paws – did not meet his eye.

"I knew you would come," he murmured. "You are fretful, Lamet. What is there to fear for you?"

Lamet stole a glance at the great leader, his tall, bony frame, his winding tail and pointed ears. "Master... What has happened here? Can it be true?"

"The Tygrine..." Disgust filled the Suzerain's voice. "The Tygrine must be stopped."

74

"Ipanel is no longer. I feel it."

"Ipanel is dead," the Suzerain confirmed. His voice was steely and unrepentant.

"How can that—"

"He was old, Lamet. He could not help us or our noble purpose."

"He was the wisest shalian in court," she replied. "Age is hardly of consequence."

"Death claimed him," said the Suzerain.

Lamet swallowed a lump in her throat. A fire coursed through her paws. "O Great One, I dare not speak, but conscience urges me to do so. I know that worse has occurred within these halls. Something unspeakable has come to pass. What exactly, I know not, but it chills me, Wise Lord. It chills me to the bone."

"Your instincts were ever strong, Lamet. We shall need them in the final battle."

"Battles, Sire... Always battles. The first battle; the great betrayal; the Tygrine."

"It is not a joke. My spies are ever alert. I have learned of the Tygrine's alliance with a band of ferals – half wild, half slaves to the whims of the hinds, their two-legged masters. Our war is with such cats – with *all* who defy the One Law. Soon my army starts its final march to victory. A great war is coming, one where every feline alive will be forced to take sides." He paused for emphasis. "The unliving too. Cats of the spirit realm; cats of the second self. Even you, Lamet.

I need to know that you shall do what your destiny requires of you, when the time comes. It may be the hardest thing you have ever done."

The young queen sighed. "Such talk of battle, of destiny... But what has this to do with Ipanel or anything else?"

"I have enlisted spirits to the mighty cause of Sa."

"Surely that is nothing new?" said Lamet. "Spirits are our most insightful advisers. Without them we would be lost. Something more has passed within these walls. If nothing has changed, then why are my paws treading on cinders? Why does my second self shudder in my chest?"

The Suzerain considered her for a moment in silence. He had not imagined that she would discover the truth. He had not expected Fiåney to share it with her. Its power was so strong in Lamet, greater than he had realized. But her nature was wilful. Would she do what was right, in the end? Could he trust her? What his teacher Ipanel had studied a lifetime to learn, Lamet had acquired without discipline or even desire. It both frustrated and impressed the great cat. The Suzerain rarely watched his subjects closely. His glance alone was of such power that it could wreak unspeakable harm by accidental contact. He had learned of old not to look too keenly with his eyes. There were different ways of seeing. The essence of a cat could be more quickly, more completely understood from smell, through sound, above all by instinct – more than the flawed sense of sight. Still, he looked at Lamet now.

In the dim light of his chamber he saw her velvety coat, slightly ruffled over her forehead. He noticed the way in which her large ears pointed out at slight angles. The fur just behind them would be at its softest, like feather down. He had a sudden impulse to touch it. He shut his eyes and the feeling passed.

"I have sent spirits to do what Mithos could not; empowered by the full moon, they shall find the Tygrine cat. They will destroy him, once and for all."

"Spirits? In Fiåney?" Lamet frowned. She did not understand.

"In Fiåney no longer," the Suzerain replied. He waited for her response. He sensed her resistance. A will quicker to challenge than obey.

Her jaw fell. "But how?"

"It is possible. There are spells that you do not yet know, Lamet. You are a sapling in Sa's endless forest. You are ignorant."

"Not so ignorant that I fail to see wrong when it confronts me."

"Beware what passes your tongue. You are but an apprentice. Your youth and status shall not protect your treason. I demand to know whom you have spoken to!"

"No living cat has entered my confidence!" insisted Lamet.

"Do not be sly with me, catling. You consort with spirits of doubtful honour, those with questionable allegiances,

77

and you think this acceptable because they are in Fiåney. You cannot know of their backgrounds, of their lineage — you cannot guess the type of cats they used to be."

"That hardly matters," returned Lamet. "When a cat becomes a spirit, they forget the waking world. Oh, they may have a passing sense of where they lived; of their amma; perhaps their favourite food, or smell — a shard of memory — but nothing more. They would not even know if they had once been loyal to the Sa Mau or the Abyssinia Tygrine!"

"Quite the expert on the dream-wake, are you not? Ipanel's teachings, I presume?" The Suzerain was dismissive. "He was not always right. Occasionally, a spirit remembers more of their mortal life. You may learn that the hard way. And even for those who have forgotten, there are new bonds forged in Fiåney daily. And so I demand to know, who have you spoken to?"

Lamet's ears flicked back. "I am no cat's fool, My Lord. And I have spoken to none of your Court."

"You have spoken to spirits! The dream-wake is my Court! Soon, the whole world shall be my empire!"

"Nobody *owns* Fiåney! Ipanel taught me that."

"Ipanel is dead," hissed the Suzerain coldly.

"He was loyal to you, My Lord. Thus would you silence others?"

"I would do what is best for the Kingdom of Sa. I always have. Yet death took Ipanel — it was not my doing."

"What is 'best' for Sa?" Lamet retorted. "You might have

78

waited to challenge the Tygrine in open combat. I could have fought him – I am ready, My Lord. Instead, you have sent forth others to slay him – spirits that no cat can defeat. And in this act, you have risked the safety of the empire! We all know of the ancient laws of nature, and yet you have disregarded them!"

"Cease," growled the Suzerain. His voice was low but threatening, carrying the tang of something acidic.

Lamet flinched. Steeling herself, she replied. "You tell me that Ipanel's death was not by your design but I feel his shock and betrayal – it tarries in your chamber. It screams of gross injustice: that you have released spirits against the laws of nature – spirits that should exist in Fiåney alone. And now they roam the physical realm. What harm may they do in their quest for the Tygrine?"

"The Tygrine must be stopped!" roared the Suzerain.

"At what cost, Master?"

"Enough!" he yowled. "You *shall* not disobey me! I will not hear of such rebellion, not even from you! My actions will not be questioned! One more word out of you and I will—"

"What would you do? Have me killed? Have me killed like Ipanel?" She lifted her face, glaring defiantly at the Cat Lord.

Quaking with anger, the Suzerain opened his eyes. Lamet gasped, stumbling back. Darkness poured over her, reaching inside her. She could feel something precious – something vital – drain from her body, and she pawed the ground desperately. Her heart thundered. Her whiskers quivered and she gave a small mew.

The Suzerain wrenched his eyes away and Lamet fell back, breathing heavily.

"You have only known comfort and ease," said the Cat Lord. "You are spoilt, catling, damaged beyond hope of repair. Now you shall know misery and hardship – you shall know what it is to be an outcast. You are banished forthwith from the Kingdom of Sa. If my fighters find you, they will kill you."

Lamet stared in disbelief. She tried to speak but the shock at her clash with him was still too close, her fear too sharp.

His voice was quiet again. "Leave at once."

"But—"

"At once," he whispered.

She felt him sink into Fiåney. Her head was thumping, her paws raging with heat. She backed towards the entrance of the chamber, turned and bolted along the corridor and out into the city. Already the morning had turned muggy and airless – no trace of a breeze remained in the air. Lamet paused below the red paw of the Sa Mau, blinking away a wisp of dust, fighting against a tremor of panic. The Court had been her life since kittenhood. It was the only world she had ever known. How would she survive outside it?

The Journey Upstream

Mati awoke to the blissful smell of chicken. He had not meant to sleep for long, but on opening his eyes he saw that the sun was already climbing over the city. Strings of shabby terraces rose around the far bank, but these ended abruptly and fashionable glass apartment blocks took over. Wooden decking skirted the apartments and, at intervals, teak boxes enclosed rows of fuchsias, geraniums and busy Lizzies. The greenery had been carefully managed. Mati's whiskers twitched. From where he sat, not even a sprig of grass was visible. His eyes trailed up the angular apartments. Sitting at one of the high windows, a Burmese cat was watching the ferals curiously. Her eyes locked on Mati and she rose to her paws on the windowsill. Staring back at her, he felt the echo of her voice, all of a rush.

"I am lonely," her eyes told him. "Who are you?" she silently asked. "All those cats ... I have never seen so many cats... They don't let me out. I live here, inside. It is dangerous outside. There are cat-thieves outside. And foxes. They feed me here. They look after me. They don't let me out..."

The Burmese gazed at Mati. He looked away, saddened. His gaze drifted over stooping terraces that led to the apartments. He concluded that these old buildings would not last much longer – for reasons that he couldn't begin to fathom, the humans did not want them any more.

They like new things, thought Mati. They don't like to remember what has gone before. When something gets old, the hinds destroy it – they wipe it out and start again.

This insight made him ponder humans and their whims. Long generations of history – of war, malice and suspicion – weighed upon the Tygrine cat. He liked the idea of eliminating the old: of starting afresh.

The other cats were rising with silent yawns. They had slept for several hours among the bicycles, curled closely against one another for warmth and comfort.

"Look at this!" Sparrow enthused, nudging a chicken drumstick towards Mati. "Pangur and Sinestra found a market nearby. They got away with a hearty plunder!"

Mati looked up. There were several pieces of meat piled at the end of the bicycle shelter nearest the river, and the ferals were sharing these around. He sniffed the drumstick. "Is this for us?" he asked.

"Yes, my boy, it is!" Sparrow licked his lips.

"It's a nice bit." Mati stared at it doubtfully. Wouldn't the alphas want it for themselves? Mati was still a catling, yet to grow into an adult tom. In the world of the ferals, with all its hierarchy, it felt strange to receive special privileges – even though he knew that he was different from the others.

"It would seem that you are valued," the ginger tom returned. "Best not to question gifts from on high but to gladly accept them!" Sparrow's good eye sparkled, while the other squinted slightly. A rumbling purr escaped his throat. "Shall we tuck in here? You know I do not stand on ceremony where food is concerned!"

Mati did know – Sparrow was a cat who prized food above all else. The catling shot a look past the bicycle shed. Ahead of them was a car park, behind which rose warehouses. People in overalls were milling around in the distance. "Let's eat it over there where no one can see us."

"Right you are!" Sparrow gripped the drumstick with his teeth and followed Mati. With the first bite of chicken, the catling relaxed. The world had not, after all, changed overnight. The sun caught his whiskers and warmed his wet nose; the kittens, Pips and Scallion, batted the long grasses bordering the near bank of the river; and there was nothing quite like chicken in the morning.

Once the cats had finished breakfast, they gathered behind the bicycle shed to discuss their next move. Pangur sat in the middle with Mati by his side. The others crowded round.

"Today we keep walking," Pangur began. He caught Mati's eye. "We continue to follow the river upstream."

This was received with miaowing protests.

"We're tired!" cried Arabella. "We've already walked most of the night and strayed far away from the Territory!"

"We really should be thinking about going back now," Torko agreed.

Pangur's eyes flashed with impatience. "We're not going back."

"Not ever? But surely—"

"Who here dares speak about 'ever'? Not now, that much is certain." The chief's tail swished. "Didn't you listen to a word I said at the meeting?"

"So where are we going?" asked Kroof. "What are we trying to reach?"

Pangur turned to Mati. "I think you need to answer that."

Mati's ears flattened. "We're ... we're not trying to *reach* anywhere. Not somewhere in particular."

The cats miaowed so loudly at Mati's response that Pangur glanced nervously towards the distant warehouses, watching out for curious humans. The tom narrowed his eyes. Cocking his head he whispered in Mati's ear, "You will have to do better than that!"

Mati swallowed. What *could* he tell them? It wasn't as though he had anywhere in mind as their destination – he just wanted to be as far as possible from Cressida Lock, with its lengthening shadows.

"What I mean," said Mati, "is that we need to get away from the Territory. There is something bad out there. It is heading for the lock. I think it might already be there."

"Already be there?" echoed Sinestra, her voice tight.

"Bad like Mithos?" asked Domino. Mati had slain the Sa's assassin, just when it had seemed as though all was lost, but the fear of the cruel-hearted cat still haunted the ferals.

Mati nodded.

"But Mithos is dead," said Ria, her silvery coat twitching. "Isn't he...?"

"It's not Mithos. But I sense that the same dark force is at work again. Cats of the Sa Mau. The Suzerain..."

Ria's eyes grew wide. "What do they want?"

"I'm not sure." He paused, thoughts growing muddled. "Maybe it's more true to say I don't know why. I think they want me gone. It goes back to the first great battle between my tribe and the cats of the Sa Mau. The Sa won't tolerate me, a Tygrine. They despise us." Again, Mati felt shame rise from every fibre of his fur – it was his fault that the company was in danger; it was he that the Suzerain wanted. A sense of guilt weighed on him, even though he knew that he had done nothing wrong; that the Tygrines had been victims of the pitiless Sa. Where did so much hostility stem from? What could he do in the face of such hate?

"They'll have to get past me first!" declared Domino, craning his neck forward and glaring like a warring tom.

Mati blinked at his loyal friend. How could this kind-natured market cat be expected to resist the dark power of the Suzerain? What if he came to harm? A thought occurred to Mati. He could leave, alone, unseen. He could disappear. The others would be safe that way – the Sa had no fight with them.

"So we keep moving, in order to escape whatever it is that is following you, or following us," said Trillion. "But when do we stop? We need a territory, we need land – a cat is not nomadic. We were not meant to wander for ever."

"For ever?" scoffed Pangur. "We have walked but a night. This is nothing compared with the escapades of a young tom. I myself travelled long distances before I reached Cressida Lock and settled down. I and my brother." He paused. His brother Hanratty had been killed by Mithos. The cats blinked in respect. "We shall keep walking until Mati deems it safe to stop." Pangur spoke resolutely, black coat glittering with light, fire glinting in his eyes. No one challenged him. He glanced at Mati and the catling knew at that moment what it was to have friends, to be trusted and respected.

Hold on to this feeling, a sudden impulse told him: it cannot last.

Mati remembered his earlier insight: that when something grew old, humans destroyed it – they wiped it out and started again. At first, he had liked the idea of deleting history, but now as he thought of it his tail sank to the ground.

Nothing lasted. It was only the beginning of autumn but already the leaves of the trees were turning yellow, rustling, growing rigid in the breeze. Soon they would fall and the trees would be bare. Flowers were wilting; bulbs slept beneath chilly soil. Winter was coming.

They set off again late that morning, following the path of the river. Pangur was insistent that they shouldn't be seen by humans, who would question the reason for a group of wandering cats, and who might try to stop them. Torko told tales of feline compounds built by human hands, where cats without collars were rounded up and imprisoned. With this chilling warning in mind, the ferals resolved to keep a low profile – although few were sure what to believe. In any case, it was a fact known to all that humans were not to be trusted – even the friendly ones could suddenly turn on a cat, seemingly without reason. As far as possible, the ferals walked the wildest stretches of the riverbank, straying through tall grasses and latticing weeds.

Mati's senses extended along the riverbank in both directions, detecting the presence of scuttling mice and blackbirds pecking for worms beneath nearby hedges. He tried to identify the scent of dogs, of prowling tomcats or nearby humans. Occasionally, he altered their path away from the riverbank, due to a seen or sensed obstruction.

After some initial chitchat, the cats stalked on in silence. Sparrow, who had been entertaining Pips and Scallion with his tale of the happy tuna, had abandoned his efforts. Being a cat of advanced years and considerable girth, he struggled to keep up with the kin. The kittens took to leaping at the legs of unsuspecting ferals, much to their mother's embarrassment.

When the sun reached its highest point, the cats sat to rest near some industrial rubbish bins. There were pigeons foraging nearby and two of the queens went hunting. The other ferals sat lazily washing themselves in the sun.

Ever watchful, Mati glanced around. He stood on a square of concrete a short distance from his friends. The sun touched individual blades of grass, lighting them with gold. Beyond the grass lay the restless river, winding its way from Cressida Lock and onwards to the sea. Mati's paws tingled. He froze, concentrating. He thought he could feel a gentle drumming from the ground. Frowning, he tried to identify the cause of the vibrations – could it be distant traffic? Some sort of machine? He wasn't sure. The more he tried to feel it, the less certain he became that it was there at all. The wind had changed direction to drift downstream and it was harder to tell what lay behind them. He closed his eyes but sensed no one on their trail. Still, he felt the urge to keep moving. He opened his eyes. If they kept going now, how far could they get by nightfall?

Pangur shook his head, catching the look on the Tygrine's face. "The cats are tired. They must rest. We cannot keep walking without a break."

"I know," said Mati, "it's just…" His voice trailed away.

"We will start again soon. For now, take a break and relax while you can."

"Thank you, Mr Pangur, sir." Mati went to sit near Domino. His legs were tired and he stretched with relief. A nagging doubt persisted. Had something picked up their scent on the afternoon breeze? A group of cats might avoid the notice of unsuspecting humans, but a vigilant tom would be quick to catch their trail. Were they being tracked?

"Amma, is it true that hinds don't like offerings of birds?" asked Scallion, as his sister Pips pranced at a wilting dandelion as if it was a mouse.

Pritin leaned over and started washing Scallion roughly behind the ears. She was used to the perpetual questions of the kittens and generally ignored them.

"Is it, Amma, is it?" Pips pursued, losing interest in the dandelion and gambolling towards her brother. The flower's pollen dusted her nose and she sneezed. Pritin looked up with a disapproving frown that warned "you next!" and continued to wash Scallion.

"It is very true, my kit, very true," piped up Sparrow. "It remains a mystery to me why any cat would own. Hinds can be so, well, *ungrateful*." He shook his ginger head. "They are such complex creatures. Sometimes they want attention, I hear, and other times they wish to be left alone, but even the shalians couldn't guess at their changing desires!"

Mati caught the word "shalian" and instantly recalled

Etheleldra and her hollow oak. He had heard her calling him through the dream-wake, warning him to flee the market-place. Where was she now?

"What, even gifts?" Pips was asking Sparrow. "Don't hinds like gifts?" She trotted round to the old ginger cat, stubby tail raised and trembling cheerfully. "I like gifts! Amma got us a vole once, she caught it by the river, remember, remember Amma how you gave us a vole?"

"You scarcely touched it," muttered Pritin.

"Ah yes, the gifts," Sparrow recalled. "No, indeed. They do not seem fond of presents of any kind, no matter how lavish, or how laboured the process of obtaining the delectable prize. Not even tasty offerings like birds and mice!"

Beneath his mother's washing tongue, Scallion gasped dramatically. "How can anyone *not* want a bird? Or a mouse? I could eat a whole mouse, all by myself!"

"Indeed?" Sparrow eyed the kitten doubtfully. "Well, I have heard tell that hinds reject such gifts, even shouting cruel insults at the cat who dutifully bestows them. A strange and might I add discourteous response to a generous bequest!"

"That's nothing," scoffed Pips, ignoring Sparrow and responding to her brother's claims about his voracious appetite, "I could eat a whole blackbird!"

"No you couldn't!"

"Could too!" Pips licked her lips.

"Enough, both of you!" snapped Pritin. "Come and have

some milk." At this invitation, the kittens scrambled eagerly to her side and started to drink, their clumsy, wedge-shaped paws kneading against her, their voices rising in satisfied purrs.

Mati watched them, recalling his earliest days with his mother. Nearby sat Sparrow, the kindly ginger tom who had taken him in at Cressida Lock. Mati's gaze shifted to Pangur, the young Cressida chief. His temper was short; he could be unpredictable. Yet the chief had trusted Mati, whose counsel he followed without question, and he had lost most of his kin in the process. And here, by Mati's side, was his loyal friend Domino, sleeping peacefully, whiskers quivering. A wave of affection rushed over Mati. His heart already ached for these cats. Soon he would have to steal out alone; to betray them; to lose them. He would walk with the ferals for now, walk until he found somewhere safe for the kin to rest and build a home. Then he would leave them.

The Bramble Fortress

Mati sank into sleep, through dreams and beyond them, towards the halls of Fiåney. He started to pull back, to avoid that undefined, mysterious world that seemed to carry with it such uncertainty. At the same time he longed to go there. There was a familiarity in the dream-wake that took Mati back to his first moments on earth, to half-formed days of touch and sense at his mother's side, before his eyes were open. Something even more profound recalled him to a place that existed before his birth, that he had somehow always been a part of. He could no longer bear to stay away.

Drifting gently into Fiåney's enclosing folds, he discovered a silence that could not be found in the waking world. Stillness surrounded him. He felt no breeze, no warmth or cold. Eerily, he smelled nothing – no hint of humans, or of other cats. A strange numbness seemed to enclose him.

The darkness lifted enough for him to see three passages materialize before his eyes. The air became indigo.

I have been here before, thought Mati. The dream-wake was vast, perhaps even limitless, and he wondered at how he had managed to return to this junction without even trying. What did it mean? Each passage seemed to reach towards him, beckoning, and he felt stretched: compelled to follow three different paths.

"Mati?" called a voice from the left passage. "Mati?" He held his breath. He knew that voice – had missed it with all his heart.

"Amma?" he replied. He could feel her presence, floating before him only whiskers away. Faintly he smelled uncut grass, a woody perfume of pine and cedar, of rich earth and jasmine. He heard birdsong and the sound of the wind as it played through leaves, humming, almost purring. "Amma, where are you?"

"Mati?" It was no longer his mother's voice, and it came from overhead.

Mati felt himself lifting from the halls of Fiåney, rising back to the waking world. He resisted, clinging to the dream-wake, hooking his claws into its gossamer walls. "Amma, where are you?" he called, starting down the left passage, from which he had heard his mother's voice.

"Mati, wake up! *Mati!*"

He opened his eyes.

Domino was standing over him. "You scared me!" said the harlequin catling. "I couldn't stir you. Were you dreaming?"

The Tygrine swallowed. His throat felt tight, and sadness washed over him. He tried to push away the memory of his mother. It was as though he had lost her all over again.

What *is* Fiåney? he wondered. Another realm; a different world – the world of the spirit, of the sixth sense.

Not for the first time, he considered whether the images from Fiåney could be real, or just figments of his own imagination. Were they messages? Were they warnings? He sat up and glanced over Domino's shoulder, his paw pads growing warm. The sun shone brightly overhead but far in the east, a speck of darkness pulsed like a black star.

Domino was watching him worriedly.

Mati sighed. "I was far away, it is true. But it wasn't a dream."

The cats continued their journey along the riverbank, Mati in the lead with Pangur close behind. The breeze ruffled their coats and kneaded the surface of the water. Long shadows gathered over the silent river and the ramshackle buildings that loomed beyond it.

Trillion sidled up to the chief. "I know that we have to keep moving – that we are not safe staying still too long. But the cats cannot walk day and night. We should decide how our energies are best spent. If we are safer under cover of darkness, then let us limit our movements by day."

"I agree," said Pangur. "Although I am wary of another night without the protection of a territory. If we stop, we will be easily surrounded. Or should we find somewhere to wait out the night? I have sensed many wandering toms already and sought to avoid them, and it is clear that Mati fears great peril, although he speaks little. A lone tom is no match for me, of course, but what of other hazards? It is told that foxes roam in the south of the city. They could not out-run us, but the kits..."

Overhearing this, Mati felt a chill. Perhaps it would be better to rest once dusk came, to conserve energy until the morning – to avoid the creatures that prowled the bank at night. Yet his instincts told him to keep moving through the twilight hours – that darkness carried unfathom-able danger. Reaching his senses backwards, downstream towards Cressida Lock, he tried to distinguish voices on the afternoon air. His ears flicked back. The land felt quiet. *Too quiet.*

He padded on determinedly, stepping lightly over weeds. The path along the bank tapered and eventu-ally disappeared, leaving only a narrow walkway that the cats followed. Burrs clutched at Mati's black-tipped tail. Brambles crowded round him, their deep violet blackber-ries ripening among hooked thorns. The brambles sprawled ahead in erratic twists, draping over the riverbank. Soon the path disappeared entirely beneath their arching branches.

Mati's tail twitched. To the north was Cressida Lock; to

the east the placid river. Gazing east, he saw the speck of darkness. It seemed to be clustering, swelling. He grew fearful and pressed forward.

"We cannot go that way," said Pangur, coming up behind him.

"It's fine, we can manage." Mati stepped tentatively into the bramble bush and edged his way through the branches that snatched at his legs like barbed wire.

"Don't be foolish! We will have to go round."

Mati ignored him, treading deeper between the thorns. He felt one snag his tail and flinched.

"Get out of there at once!" ordered Pangur. "I am still your chief, and I demand you come back."

Mati froze. His every movement caused the complex structure to quiver and groan. Even as he stood still, a stray thorn bobbed on a spindly branch, grazing his nose. If he, a nimble catling, could not navigate his way through the bramble bush, how would cats like Sparrow manage? Reluctantly, he backed out, his fur disarrayed.

Pangur growled. "What madness was that, young cat?" The others stood behind him, listening eagerly.

"I didn't want to go around it," said Mati sheepishly.

"Why not?"

Mati glanced about him, away from the river, but brambles blocked his view.

Something's out there, he thought, something is moving in the sky, coming closer. Who knows what it is? Perhaps it's harmless, nothing to be scared of. But I feel cold when I see it. How quickly will it reach us? And where, if not east, is there to go? We cannot cross the river, we cannot pass the thorny bush. We cannot go back.

How could he explain his instincts to the chief? He turned to the tomcat with a heavy heart. "Mr Pangur, I think you're right, although I wish there was some other way. We have no choice but to leave the riverbank: to journey east."

With a feeling of unease, Mati made his way around the creeping brambles. They spread unchecked along the western fringes of the bank, blocking access to the river as far as the eye could see. Pangur followed close behind, leading the ferals who exchanged wary glances. Several had seen Mati's attempt to pass within the thorny hedge, and they questioned his judgement.

"That cat has no sense," whispered Arabella to Torko.

Torko eyed the Tygrine suspiciously. "Never seen anything like it in my life. Heading straight into the brambles like that. Expecting us to follow. I suppose we should follow him, too, if the whim takes him to jump into the river? To seek out oolfs or to crawl inside a hornet's nest?"

Pangur shot round. He glared at Torko and Arabella, who fell silent.

The brambles seemed to signpost the borders of the city. Around them the ground was unkempt, rising towards a fallow, empty field. The last of summer's poppies dotted the edges among tall grasses, red petals limp. Thistles crouched between them, their blue flowers dry, their sharp leaves clawing the air.

Mati nosed his way between the weeds until he was standing at the start of the field. The land beneath him had been cleared of crops, soil dusting the pads of his paws. Through it, Mati realized he could feel few vibrations rising from the dry ground. The dull soil provided no echo, no murmurings of the world around them. He tried to sense the drumming of paws he had felt approaching earlier, but could only hear the surrounding ferals as they trod tentatively around him.

Beyond the fallow land, raised on a low hill deeper to the east, Mati saw a cornfield and, further away, an isolated farmhouse. For a moment, he thought that a lonely man was standing among the reaching corn, arms outstretched, a tattered hat on his head. Mati blinked. It was no man – just an eerie figure that even from this distance scarcely resembled one.

"A scarecrow," said Pangur, pausing alongside Mati. "I have heard of such things. Hinds use them to keep birds away."

Mati nodded, although he didn't really understand what humans had to fear in birds, or why a bird would be fooled by such a weak imitation of a man's frame. He was mindful of the risk of humans but felt an intense desire to leave the fallow land, this huge expanse of soil where nothing dared to grow.

He started towards the cornfield, resigned to the fact that they were leaving the river behind. He regretted their departure. In a curious way, the nearby river had made him feel safe. Walking through a large, earthy field, he was exposed. Against the backdrop of crumbling soil, there was nowhere to hide.

The cats walked in silence under the late afternoon sun. For those with keen vision, their colourful and varied coats could be seen overhead for many miles. Their shadows crept ahead of them, the tallest already tickling the borders of the field, although the owners of the shadows lagged far behind.

Mati did his best to navigate his way over the soil without stumbling. It sank into his claws and stuck to the soft fur between his pads, weighing him down. Like any cat, he felt the urge to be clean – it was all he could do not to stop and wash himself. His eyes flitted ahead of him and down to his dirty paws. He did not look up – he did not notice the dark, swirling flecks he had spotted earlier that day – did not see them drawing closer above the cornfield and distant farmhouse.

The ferals trod silently, struggling over rutted ground. Even Pips and Scallion grew tired of games. It was hard work for them to cross the field on their short legs and Pritin had to nudge them along. Noticing their difficulty, Pangur offered to carry the kittens by the scruff in turns. "Or I could take Scallion while one of the others takes Pips," he suggested.

"No, no!" cried both kittens in unison. Nothing would be more shaming than to be carried like that.

"Well, if you're sure," said Pangur with a glint in his eyes. "But stay close, don't fall behind. That goes for everyone," he added, looking across the ferals.

"They're sure," said Pritin quickly, protective of her kittens. Despite her trust in the chief, she was uneasy at the thought of any tom touching them.

The cats trudged on as afternoon wore away and the sun sank lower in the sky. Mati held the lead, with Pangur close behind. Ria, Sinestra and Kroof followed them, ahead of Trillion and Domino. Beyond, the group unravelled, with Sparrow huffing to keep up, Torko and Arabella ambling after him and Pritin trailing with Pips and Scallion.

The cornfield was drawing closer with its towering crops. They would be safe there, thought Mati, safe to rest without being seen. The sun waned to the west. As he pressed ahead, he became aware of a strange wind playing with his whiskers, warm and familiar. He felt a distant drumming through the earth, like stumbling paws across hard ground. He turned back towards the river, hidden beyond the blur of roving brambles, and was alarmed to see how far behind some of the cats had strayed. His whiskers bristled, his eyes growing wide.

"What is it?" hissed Pangur, catching the expression on Mati's face. He looked up and his jaw fell.

Mati followed his gaze. With a gasp, he noticed the

circling flecks drawing nearer.

"Hawks," breathed Pangur. "Birds that hunt other birds. I have seen one before, but never a flock."

"They eat their own kind?" Mati shuddered. The idea of cannibalism among any creatures — that a bird could stalk and feast on another bird — filled him with disgust.

"But they won't touch us," the chief assured. "They would not tackle a cat!"

Mati nodded. All the same, his heart started thumping.

Sinestra had stopped just behind them. "Look!"

"They won't touch us," Pangur repeated. "They are just birds. Stay together, keep walking slowly, we are nearly at the border of the field."

The hawks started wheeling over their heads, etching invisible circles beneath the dusky clouds. A sapphire glaze hung over the cornfield, beyond which rose the farmhouse in dark silhouette.

"These aren't just birds," uttered Trillion. "Look at their size!"

The other cats shifted nervously, eyes darting around the fallow field. There was nowhere to hide. The nearest cover was the cornfield, still many paces away. Mati stared at the circling birds, his eyes glassy. He thought he heard a quivering, clicking noise overhead — a sort of alien chatter. The birds were too far above him for their calls to be audible. And yet he sensed something of their distant voices — more than their voices — he heard, or felt, the fizz and clack of

101

their thoughts. Not words exactly, or anything that could be understood in sentences. Dark, ghoulish sounds. He pictured these noises as colours in his mind's eye: as shades of violet and splashes of lurid red.

"Keep moving, stay close together," urged Pangur. "Tuck in your tails so they've nothing to cling to. They are no match for us so long as we don't get separated. Remain calm."

Even as Pangur made this last command, Torko broke from the group, sprinting towards the cornfield. Arabella followed swiftly. The other ferals lost their nerve and started tearing across the fallow field as quickly as they could. Kroof stumbled, falling behind. Ria shot in the wrong direction.

"Don't panic!" urged Pangur, but the cats pushed past him. Only Mati stayed frozen where he stood. A black chill had seized him – a sudden, certain knowledge that these weren't ordinary birds. There was darkness at their hearts, a cruel intent beyond their own, mysterious reasoning. They were messengers of the Suzerain.

"The Sa," murmured Mati.

Domino threw a look over his shoulder. Realizing that his friend was rooted to the spot, he returned to stand at Mati's side.

Pangur and Domino stared at the Tygrine cat. The chief spoke. "What did you say?"

Mati blinked at them, breaking from his trance.

"Run!" he cried as the birds started darting towards them with horrifying speed, their beaks snapping, their hooked talons splayed. Dark feathers fluttered on the air.

Pangur, Mati and Domino bolted across the field. Earth sprayed in their eyes as they tripped over clods of soil. The birds shot after them effortlessly. One hovered above Mati's head and overtook him, its shadow sweeping over his body and darkening his path. It swooped round and dived towards him.

"Careful, Mati!" warned Domino, who had fallen a few tail-lengths behind.

Mati threw himself onto his side and twisted out of the hawk's grasp, the razor-sharp talons skimming his flank. He felt the tremor of air as it flew past him and leaped back onto his paws, completing the last stretch of the field at a sprint. He collapsed, breathless, between the lofty corn. It rose high over his head, providing camouflage and protection from the raptors' hungry beaks and their cold, searching eyes.

Domino dropped by his side. "You OK?"

"Yes," gasped Mati.

"Is everyone here?" shouted Pangur as the cats fell gasping around him.

A piercing wail tore through the air – the cry of a creature in anguish. It chilled the ferals to the bone, their fur spiking with terror. It might have been the screech of a furious hawk, or a creature from another land. It took Mati a moment to realize that a cat had made that sound – that it was Pritin.

"My kits!" she cried. "They've taken my kits!"

The Harakar

Mati sprang to his feet. Peering between the corn stems, he spotted Pritin standing alone in the fallow field. Her head was thrown back and a long, agonized wail escaped her throat. Two hawks soared overhead, clutching the terrified kittens in their talons. They lifted them towards the other birds that ducked and swirled above.

Mati took a deep breath and burst out of the cornfield, back onto the ploughed soil. He leapt clumsily towards Pritin, skidding to a halt in front of her. At first she scarcely noticed him. "I'll get them!" he told her. "I'll bring them back!"

She lowered her face, catching the Tygrine with a desperate look, fixing her eyes on his. Please, her gaze implored him as her voice still wailed in agony, please Mati, rescue my kits!

Staring back at her, Mati hesitated. It seemed to him that the entire universe rested in those bright green orbs, as though the answer to all questions floated in their glistering depths. Within them he glimpsed the verdant green of papyrus reeds with their grassy flowers and the winding river of his kittenhood. He saw his mother, who had sacrificed everything to save him, and he knew that this young queen would do the same for her kittens. The power of her devotion seemed to Mati to encompass all that was right in the world – all that was good. This thought lingered as his own eyes dimmed, as his body relaxed and he bowed his head.

Crouching at the border of the field, wet noses peeping nervously from tall necks of corn, the ferals took in a curious sight: the giant hawks circled overhead, darkening the sky, while beneath them Pritin stood erect. Her cry had subsided into a thin, breathless mewl. Before her slumped the russet-coated Tygrine, his body limp, his head lolling heavily against his front paws, as if in sleep.

But Mati was not asleep.

At first there was only silence, and acres of limitless black. Then darkness was defeated, giving way to an indigo sky. The silence was broken by chattery clacks. Mati turned his head to see a passage unfurling to his right. Darkness lay there, gilded by a crescent of violet light. Deep within the passageway, he heard the wail of a cat in pain and the crackle of gathering flames. He took a step forward, into a world of pitch and despair.

Mati's fur bristled and his heart raced. This was the dark tunnel, the passage he had avoided on his previous journeys to the dream-wake. Now he entered it of his own accord. Why was he here? For a moment, he couldn't remember. He paused. He heard the beating of heavy wings, a low hiss and a screech that might have come from a cat or even a human. Or a large, predatory bird. Recalling the reason he had entered Fiâney's vaults, Mati hurried into the shadowy passageway.

A grizzle of whispered voices rose around him; angry, malicious voices uttering words that made no sense to him:

Harakar, Harakar
Those who sleep
Deep within the silent land
Those who wander endlessly
Those whose eyes no longer see

The chanting sounded familiar – the word "Harakar" chilled Mati's blood – and he remembered in a flash the ghostly voices he had heard the night that Mithos came. The Suzerain's assassin had tried to lure Mati into Fiâney. Was this another trap devised by the Sa Mau? Mati faltered and the darkness lifted, revealing for a moment the fallow field and the image of Pritin standing alone. Her mouth was open but the cry she uttered was voiceless. The silence was haunting.

The hawks were already high overhead, carrying the kittens beyond the clouds.

This is the only way, thought Mati.

He plunged back into the dream-wake. A strong, warm wind gasped against his face, stinging his eyes. The darkness enclosed him. He walked as quickly as he dared, stepping tentatively. The clacks and screeches rose again like a tide. His paws felt damp and looking down, he saw that puddles dotted the ground. Dark red puddles. Frightened, Mati glanced back. The indigo light had vanished; the exit that led to the meeting of three passages had disappeared from view, as though he had passed an invisible gateway. He was trapped in a world of violet shadows.

The liquid within the puddles grew warmer. It singed the delicate pads of Mati's paws. The chants rose around him. Against them, he heard the long, desperate keening of a cat in pain and his heart felt as though it would break with sorrow. It was Pritin's voice, piercing through the dream-wake's walls, although in the waking world no sound escaped her throat. In Fiåney, her voice cowered, as though ensnared, and Mati feared it would stay there for ever if he didn't find her kittens. The violet haze dimmed until total blackness enveloped him. His paws throbbed with pain. The screeches of the hawks faded and only the ghoulish chants rose above Pritin's moans to echo through the darkness:

Those who wander endlessly
Those whose eyes no longer see
Ha'atta, ha'atta...

Doubt rose in Mati and he trembled with terror. How would he find the kittens in this forsaken wasteland? "Won't somebody help me?" he whimpered. "I am lost..." The thought brought back memories of his old friend Jess, and Mati staggered, the sadness overwhelming him.

"Mati?" The voice found him in the dream-wake, cutting through the whispers and chants of enemies unseen. "It is I, the spirit Bayo. Have you need of my guidance?"

Mati's ears flicked forward. The pain in his paws waned, and his body shuddered with relief. He remembered Bayo. A friend, he recalled – a good spirit: someone he could trust.

"Thank you, wise spirit," said Mati. His voice drifted back to him. In Fiåney it sounded different – deeper, stronger, despite his immaturity and doubt. "I do need guidance. I am lost, lost in this horrible place. I have to find Pritin's kits. Birds took them. Giant birds. They lifted them into the sky!"

"They are taking them to *him*," Bayo uttered, his voice dropping to a whisper. "They are taking them to the Cat Lord. They were meant to take you."

"To the Suzerain?" gasped Mati.

"Do not call him by this name," the spirit berated. "Do not tempt his attentions. Already his high priests are chanting

109

his spells. Do you not hear them? Where they lead, he soon shall follow."

Mati swallowed hard, panic coursing through him. Again, others were suffering on his account. He should have left the ferals sooner, as he had planned. It was his fault... "Have you seen the birds, Mr Spirit?"

"Keep going, Mati. For they have risen high out of your reach now, high over the waking world, and only in Fiåney shall you find them. Find the hawks and kill them! Without hesitation, for they are the servants of evil devices."

"Kill them?" The words hung damply. "But this is Fiåney. Surely I can't... Wouldn't I need to cross to the physical realm? The world of the first self?"

"Kill or be killed – of course it is possible here. You think they cannot make you bleed?"

Mati trembled, his breath catching in his throat. He knew instinctively that this was true – that the feline spirit could die here, in this lonely place, and leave the body to perish, just as the death of the body might extinguish the second self. Hadn't he sensed as much when Mithos had stalked him in this realm?

Bayo continued, "If they can hurt you, you can hurt them. With one exception." He paused a moment, and when he spoke there was the murmur of humour in his voice. "You could not kill *me*, whatever I might do to you. I am a spirit."

"Etheleldra said that spirits are something like ghosts."

"Yes, perhaps. A ghost – a phantom. You cannot kill a

phantom. You cannot kill what does not live."

Mati's fur spiked at the back of his neck.

"Forget that, catling," said Bayo. "These birds are no spirits – they are servants of Fiåney but born of a physical presence. Kill them you can, and must. Take courage in your own power."

"Power? Even here, in this terrible place?"

"This 'place'..." the spirit's voice grew soft and for a moment Mati thought he had departed. Then he spoke again. "This 'place' is the Harakar. It is the world that was, even before the Creators came, before the sun conquered the armies of the night. It is the darkland, yes, the realm beyond the first dark gate. Despite that it is still within Fiåney. Which means it is yours to explore. The Cat Lord uses it, draws from it, but it is not his to claim. No more than it is yours. No more than it is any cat's. Still, I urge you not to delay. His powers surge through the Harakar. Amid the chaos, he is boldest. He may come in search of you, if you tarry here too long. He is far away to risk it, perhaps, his first self concealed in his secret palace. And yet he desires to see you, to destroy you – desires it with all his heart. Who knows what perils he shall run to fulfil this lust? Hurry, Mati. Find the kits and return to the waking world." The voice faded.

"Please, Mr Spirit, sir – please guide me! Where are the kits?"

"Go now, all speed," the voice told him, waning against

111

the rising chants, the curses and yowls of the Harakar.

Trapped in a mantle of darkness, without signpost or directions, Mati found that his legs were racing beneath him, splashing through the low, scorching pools, almost unbidden. His paws flew over the ground, seeking a path with a confidence that surprised him. Against the eerie chants, and Pritin's desperate mewl, Mati heard the clatter and clacks of the hawks. With a burst of energy, he lunged after them.

The Harakar flushed red and he knew that he was close. Still he kept running. A smell of burning wafted his way. The warm wind jostled against him, hindering him, stinging his eyes and forcing back his ears. Sound distorted. Feathers darted towards him, smacking his face. It only made him more determined and he ran on, heedless.

As he drew closer he heard the thoughts of Pips and Scallion, dizzy in the grip of the hawks, high over the sky. "Help us," they cried, "the birds are taking us! Help us, please help us!"

Mati burst through a storm of feathers and fell upon one of the leering birds. It screeched as he caught it, plunging his fangs into its throat, raking the creature with his hind claws until it fell limp. But where were the kittens? Mati leapt over the slain hawk and caught another of the flock. Bayo's words echoed in his mind: "Find the hawks and kill them!" Throwing his paws around its neck, he brought it down, scratching and tearing feathers that tasted of sour dust. Crazed, Mati fought through the screeching birds. He tore and bit like a wild cat. He sensed the kittens were whiskers away. The birds that carried them darted from him but the Tygrine had tasted blood and he would not stop now.

One of the hawks clutched Pips in its talons. Mati sank his teeth into its wing, feeling the bones crack between his jaws.

This is what happens! Mati thought in delirium. This is what happens when you taunt a Tygrine cat!

He let go of the wing, remembering the kitten. The hawk shrieked and released Pips, just as Mati closed his teeth around her scruff. The last of the hawks was less than a tail-length away. Still grasping Pips, Mati struck it with a powerful bat of the paw, sinking his claws beneath its feathers and raking them over its chest. Scallion fell from the bird's clutches with a terrified miaow and Mati shot after him, locking a front paw around the kitten and tumbling to the ground to land with a stagger, heavily but unhurt.

With a jolt he was awake, sitting in the fallow field and shaking with fury and exhaustion. It took a moment for Mati to orient himself, to understand where he was and what had happened. Above him, evening had arrived and the moon rose amid a cloudy sky. A short distance in front of him Pritin purred and pirruped euphorically, gripping her kittens gently with her paws and washing their small faces. Scattered in a circle around them were the bodies of the hawks, their necks broken, mounds of blood and feathers. Mati took in their twisted forms with huge, golden eyes. He had entered the Harakar, the chaos, had dragged Pips and Scallion back to the waking world. But had it really been him? The Tygrine of the Harakar had been merciless: a killer. Mati didn't recognize himself as that cat.

His fur smelled bitter, touched by smoke. The tang of sour blood caught on his tongue and he shivered. His body showed no outward sign of injury. But the fire of the Harakar had somehow scorched him from within, had touched his second self and had left him hollow.

The cats followed Mati in silence as he wove his way between the corn. No one approached the young cat, not even Pangur. The Tygrine was darkly aloof, haunted by the knowledge of a world that the others did not share. The ferals had taken in the broken bodies of the hawks in shock – what sort of cat would kill a bird that size? What sort of cat could kill *so many*? And how had he done it? In a trance, he had crouched in the fallow field, had stayed like that for a long time. As he had woken, the birds had dropped dead from the sky and the kittens were by his side, hurrying to the safety of their mother's embrace.

The ferals had left the fallen hawks where they lay in the fallow field, too scared to approach them. Under cover of darkness, they slunk alongside the farmhouse. Beyond it stood a deserted barn. The doors were padlocked but a gap between them was just big enough for a full-grown cat to creep through. Once inside, they lay down between bales of straw. Later, the hunters among them would go in search of mice – they had already heard plenty of them scurrying through the cornfield. For now, the kin would rest. The long day had exhausted them.

Soon the ferals slept, lost to mysterious dreams where each cat travels alone. Mati sat a short distance from the others, strained and pensive, too tired to think clearly but too disturbed to sleep. Who am I? he wondered. The catling he had thought he was had not even killed so much as a starling. He could hardly remember slaying the hawks, could scarcely recall his journey into the Harakar. But he felt with great sadness that a part of him had stayed in that sinister place – that it would remain there for ever.

He lowered his head, his senses drained. Perhaps this was why he failed to detect the drumming of paws drawing closer until they had reached the cornfield. Raising his head, his instincts suddenly alert but his mind confused, Mati's heart leapt with fright. Instantly, he was on his feet, crackling with energy. He recalled the juddering movement he had felt at Cressida Lock, at the coming of some untold terror.

A wind rose over the cornfield, lifting the wooden doors. *Smack!* went the doors against the frame: *Smack! Smack!* Still, the ferals slept, curled against bales of straw. The doors lifted, fell, lifted again and in the moment that the wind dropped, Mati sensed a familiar presence. His hairs stood like needles along his back. Silent as a ghost, the shadow of a cat had slunk through the gap in the door. It froze in the half-light, scanning the forms of the sleeping ferals. Searching. Mati's heart raced and his breath died on his tongue. The figure took a step forward, its green eyes darting across the barn. Then they rested on Mati.

The
Second
Gate

A Question of Loyalty

Lamet had scarcely stopped moving since leaving the Suzerain's court, snatching scraps of sleep in the shade along polluted side streets, under cool archways, by overflowing bins. Like a common alley cat, she thought wryly. She spoke to no one, keen to make progress – to get out of the city of Zagazig and beyond the reaches of the Empire of Sa, where every casual feline glance awoke her sense of danger. Had street cats been enlisted by the Sa? Was she being followed?

Even once she had passed the borders of the empire, Lamet struggled to relax. An unshakeable fear had stirred in her that morning in the Suzerain's chamber. She had sensed – had instinctively known – that terrible forces had been roused from Fiåney. Three creatures had escaped the dream-wake's vaults into the waking world. Ipanel had failed to stop the Cat Lord, and she had arrived too late.

Spirits from Fiåney, freed into our realm, thought Lamet. *Too late.*

Her ears flicked back as she watched a dark-skinned man with a white turban brush the fabric of his gown as he passed her. Noticing Lamet, the man paused, uttered a word and extended his hand. She blinked at him with her unusual eyes, one green, the other golden. Then she backed away, hurrying along the street and disappearing into the grounds of a mosque. She trod lightly over the cool tiles, across a felt carpet and behind a stone pillar. There, in a pall of shadow, she released herself to Fiåney.

Through the dark haze of the dream-wake, she softly called a name: "Obelghast?" She frowned as heat rose from her paws. "Dear spirit Obelghast, are you here?"

The voice that greeted her was husky, as though awakened from a long sleep. "Lamet, you seek my counsel?"

"I do, wise spirit. Trouble stirs in the waking world. Perhaps in the dream-wake too..." She glanced around blindly into the darkness.

"Yes," the spirit murmured.

"The Cat Lord has—"

Obelghast interrupted. "Do not say it. The dream-wake has ears and eyes of its own."

Lamet shivered. "But you know of what I speak."

"The Three," whispered the spirit. "The Three have been released."

120

"Yes. I fear the harm they may cause in the waking world."

"I cannot help in matters of the living – you know that. I am bound to Fiåney, to the pillars of cat, to the journey of the second self."

"But perhaps there is something you can do. Maybe you will learn of a way to prevent the evil that is at work."

"Are you asking me to take sides?"

"Of course not!" Lamet hastily put in. "Only ... I fear that Ipanel was right: this path is hazardous, harmful, not just for the Tygrine enemy – to our cause too."

"The Great Spirit would not agree with you," murmured Obelghast. "She herself assisted in the release of the Three."

"I do not doubt that. Yet you must see that their entrance to our world is fraught with danger. It is against nature."

"Neither tribe may command me." The gravelly voice of the spirit was resolute. "I will *not* take sides."

"I know, wise spirit," said Lamet. "You are one of the few who resists allegiances. It is rare in these times. That is why I trust you most of all."

"You trust one without loyalty? How can that be?"

"It makes perfect sense to me, dear spirit. You refuse to bow to Tygrine or Sa. You are incorruptible."

The spirit made a noise – almost like a stifled purr. "And you, young cat, are persuasive. But what would you have me do? I cannot defy the Great Spirit."

Lamet spoke quickly. "I am not asking for defiance. In truth, I do not know what to hope for. If there is any way

121

you can avert this disaster... If there is *anything* you can do."

"The Three are in your world now — in the land of the flesh. I do not see what a lowly spirit in Fiåney can achieve."

"You are surely not lowly, dear Obelghast! And there may be an opportunity. I beg you to be watchful. My time in the dream-wake must be short — I do not feel safe in the physical realm. I cannot leave my body unattended. You could be my senses in Fiåney. You told me that the dream-wake has ears and eyes of its own — but so do you."

"It was the Cat Lord's will that the Three be released. Remember that!" said Obelghast.

"I have not forgotten," said Lamet sadly.

"Let us say that I agree to watch the dream-wake on your behalf, that I see something in Fiåney — something that worries me. What if I cannot reach you? If you do not plan to visit here much, that is possible. And what if my deeds could compromise the cause of the Sa Mau or anger the Cat Lord? Surely, you would not wish me to act in such circumstances?"

Lamet spoke softly. "I trust you, Obelghast. You will know what to do."

"That is hardly an answer."

"Please, wise spirit," urged the young queen. Her ears twitched and she glanced furtively over her shoulder, fearing spies but seeing nothing.

"Very well," he conceded. "Lamet, it is hard to refuse you. I will listen at the Borderlands. I will see what I can glean.

If I can help, I shall. But without pledging loyalty to either tribe."

"And I assure you I would not wish you to. How could I urge fealty when I myself am so confused?" She spoke carefully, avoiding any direct reference to the Suzerain or her banishment, taking heed of Obelghast's warning that they might be overhead. "A great deal has happened since last we spoke. My status has ... *changed*. I do not beg loyalty to a tribe. What side would I ask of you?"

"You are still a cat of the Sa Mau, are you not?" said the spirit.

Lamet paused before replying. "I am," she sighed. "Even now, I am."

Night had settled over the city of Zagazig, with its hodge-podge of houses and its dusty streets. It brought no escape from the dizzying heat. A scarlet light swept across the sky, daubing the waning moon. The Commander in Chief of the Army of the Sa Mau blinked away the dust. He jumped onto a broken stone amid the rubble of the cordoned-off Old City. Before him stood dozens of cats in tidy rows. Silently, they awaited instructions.

The Commander cleared his throat. "One Law," he began. "One Law for all cat-kind!"

The officers raised their heads, eyes glistening with excitement.

"You are the guardians of the old feline order," he

continued. "You will lead the empire into brave new lands. The fighters at your command shall be countless. One Law, one empire across the world!"

The officers miaowed and cheered.

"In the moons that follow there will be call for great bravery; for courage and sacrifice. Everywhere, you will be met by treachery, by cowardice, apathy and weakness. By feline impostors – animals that deserve not the good name of cat, that have forgotten Te Bubas and all that she stands for."

The officers hissed.

"You will encounter cats who root through trash! Who live on discarded and rotting meats! Cats who scavenge, beg and steal!"

Several of the officers yowled.

"Cats who share their quarters with hinds!"

More officers joined in, cursing and spitting.

"Cats who share their quarters with *oolfs*!"

This was too much for the officers, who shrieked in disgust, their long tails swishing and their narrow backs arching.

The Commander's voice rose, his mouth widening to reveal his fangs. "In this realm and the next, we shall not be defeated! Glory to those who serve the Sa! Death to the Tygrines and traitors! Death to those who live as thieves! Long live the Suzerain, long live the Sa!"

"Long live the Suzerain, long live the Sa!" the officers cheered beneath a blood-red moon.

Old Friends

The wind had fallen, its thin voice sighing across the pastures and touching the corn in the nearby field. The door of the barn lay slack against its hinges. Silence gathered over the sleeping ferals.

Mati stared in wonder as the shadow crouching by the door rose to its feet and moved towards him, at first with faltering steps. He recalled that light-pawed tread as from a dream, and with a sense of awe those sparkling, pale green eyes. A tinkling caught the air, the faintest sigh like wind through bluebells.

"Is it really you?" His voice caught in his throat, escaping as barely a whisper.

"No one else," she replied nervously, her front paw hovering for a moment, frozen with excitement and doubt.

A shaft of moonlight touched the felt of her fur, the

sweeping patchwork of tortoiseshell-and-white.

Doubt left him then. "Jess!" he cried as he sprang towards her, shunting her amiably to the ground, washing her face, rubbing his head against hers, his heart bursting with joy. His purr rumbled thickly and he could scarcely breathe in his excitement as she nudged and pawed him, hugging his head with her agile paws, nipping him playfully behind the ears and washing his russet face.

Their *pirrups* awoke the ferals, who shrugged off a bewildered sleep. They gaped, dumbstruck. The catlings were encircling each other with ears forward and noses close, almost touching. They recognized the young queen as the one they had called the stray; the housecat who had never fitted in; who had gone home with her hind; who had returned to Cressida Lock to protect her friend.

Mati hardly noticed the kin. "You're so tall!" he told Jess.

"Really?" she purred, burying her face in the nape of his russet neck.

"Have I grown?" he asked her.

Jess stepped back, narrowing her pale green eyes. "Your face has!" she purred. It was true, too – a tom's face broadened with time. With a thickening at his cheeks, the Tygrine catling was showing the first signs of maturity.

Mati caught the teasing lilt to her voice. "Oolf!" he cried. "Snout of an oolf, you always were!" He sprang at her with a gentle bound and the catlings rolled against the floor of the barn, their purrs mingling in the still air.

126

* * *

Mati awoke with a start. In those first, confused seconds of wakefulness he felt a wave of elation without remembering why. He blinked. The other ferals were sitting or standing nearby in the barn, stretching, washing themselves and chatting. Torko was in conversation with Sparrow, telling him about the sleeping arrangements at his old territory, when he was a Kank. "Good times," he was saying. "Not grand though, not like Cressida Lock. We slept in that building, the ancient one that was falling apart. A bit dusty but plenty of space. We didn't have anything like the catacombs. Now they really are something."

Mati's muscles throbbed. The journey into the Harakar had exhausted him and even his long sleep had failed to revive him. He scanned the kin. Trillion and Pangur were standing at a distance, talking quietly. Talking about him, Mati guessed. Pangur caught the Tygrine watching and paused.

Mati's elation faded; the sense of limitless happiness waned. His eyes trailed over the ferals. One by one they fell silent. He watched them, perplexed. He noticed Pritin nearby, reclined with her kittens. She blinked at him kindly. The other cats stared at him, green eyes emerging from furry faces: tabby stripes; ginger flecks. No tortoiseshell-and-white. Had he just imaged Jess's arrival? Had he seen her in Fiåney? Where was she? He couldn't remember drifting off but he must have been sleeping for a long time.

127

Scanning the faces of the ferals, Mati's eyes rested on Domino. "She's outside," said the harlequin catling.

Mati nodded. Tail lowered, he slunk past the cats and eased his way through the gap in the door of the barn. He stepped into a damp morning. The sky was grey and drizzling. An untarred pathway led away from the barn. Tractor treads left patterns in the damp soil. The grass around the barn had been trodden down and looked dusty where it grew at the borders of the driveway. Against this, Mati spotted a shock of ginger, black and white, impossibly bright amid the gloom. Happiness coursed through him.

She turned with a trill as he approached.

"I've missed you so much, Jess, so much!" He sprang from one burst of grass to another, his tail shooting straight above him, quivering with delight.

"I've missed you too, old friend."

They circled each other, as they had the night before, purring and rubbing noses.

"When I woke up just now..." Mati blinked at her. "I thought I might have dreamt of your return. Or seen you in Fiåney... I can't believe you're really here!" He dived onto the ground, rolled over and kicked his legs in the air.

"You're like a kit!"

"I feel younger all of a sudden," he agreed. "How did you find us?"

"So many cats aren't hard to track," said Jess. She sat and began to wash herself.

"But what about your hind?" asked Mati. "Won't he miss you?"

Jess raised her face a moment. Their eyes met and he winced. He felt a surge of sadness. He pictured his friend bowing over a human face, as pale and languid as the moon. He heard human voices raised in anger, a child's entreaty, a mother's refusal. He pictured a small cage with a handle waiting by the front door of a house as a tortoiseshell-and-white cowered fearfully beneath a bed. He looked away.

Frowning, Jess stood up. "You have seen it. You have seen what happened. You read it in my eyes."

Mati nodded. "Your hind..." He cleared his throat. "The old hind. He has passed from this world."

Jess dipped her head. "What else have you seen?"

"That you found no comfort with others. That they were not kind," he said quietly. "The young one begged to keep you but her mother refused." Anger coursed through him. How could humans treat his friend so shamefully?

"My hind's daughter does not care for cats," said Jess frostily. "She tried to trap me, to take me away, to force me into the carrier. I escaped. I reached Cressida Lock but there was no sign of you." She paused, eyeing Mati curiously.

"I suppose Binjax told you that he's the new chief?" Mati didn't wait to hear her reply. "He just refused to leave the Territory and lots of the others stayed with him. I didn't think it was safe, but you know Binjax – he doesn't listen.

I thought Pangur would be angry but he acted like he didn't care what they did. Maybe I worry too much."

Jess glanced nervously over her shoulder.

"What is it, Jess?"

She turned back to him, her green eyes wide yet suddenly unreadable. "You are tired," she said at length. "Why are you so tired?"

Mati looked down at his paws. "They didn't tell you? About last night?"

"I haven't really spoken to the others."

Memories of the hawks filled Mati with repulsion: the rage that had consumed him in the Harakar; his lust to kill.

Jess must have sensed something of this, as her intense gaze softened. "Are you thirsty? There's another barn, not far from here, with milking cows."

"What are they?" asked Mati. He had never seen a cow.

"Giant beasts, but timid. They make the most delicious milk. I had some on my way here. It was easy, there were puddles of the stuff that the hinds hadn't mopped up. It's still early. No hinds around. We could get some."

"Milk?" said Mati, licking his lips, grateful for the distraction.

Jess's ear flicked back. "Last one there's an oolf's snout!"

The catlings tore through dewy fields as the first hint of sunlight lit the distant city.

Danger in the Borderlands

It was drizzling again when the ferals slunk away from the barn, with its nearby farmhouse. They had all managed to drink a little milk from the cattle shed, careful not to tread too close to the huge, placid cows with their sombre faces and rolling dark eyes. The cats walked tentatively, light footed, trailing wordlessly away from the fallow field and down towards the river.

Pangur assumed the lead but Mati and Jess walked close behind, trailed by Domino and Trillion. Some of the other cats exchanged glances – where would this journey take them? They were not used to wandering aimlessly and their paws were sore. The damp weather didn't help either.

"A cat shouldn't be out in this," Torko grumbled. "I fancy a warm chamber in the catacombs, and a good long sleep. Perhaps after some roast chicken."

Sparrow nodded dreamily. He was a cat of simple pleasures, and walking in a drizzly morning wasn't one of them. Then he remembered Mati's warning, and the incident with the poison, and he glanced at the young Tygrine who was further ahead. "Nothing to be done," he wheezed. "Need to get to safety."

"But where *is* safety?" hissed Sinestra. She was just behind them and had listened to their exchange.

The low wind tumbled downhill, and with it the ferals' words. Mati glanced at Jess, frowning.

"Ignore them," she said. "They're fools. They haven't got a clue."

Mati nodded but his tail edged round his flank and he looked away.

Pangur glanced at him.

"Mati will show us," Sparrow was saying. "Mati knows where we're going."

"He saved my kittens!" Pritin agreed. "He is a hero. Songs shall be written in his honour. New kins founded in his name!"

Sinestra sighed irritably. "Really?" she said flatly. "Such admirable faith you have in that catling. Blind faith, some might say."

Kroof murmured agreement. Arabella and Torko nodded enthusiastically. They walked beside the tabbies, exchanging glances.

Pangur stopped suddenly, causing Domino to stumble into the chief's flank.

132

"Mr Pangur, sir, I'm so sorry!" spluttered the harlequin catling.

Pangur ignored him, glaring beyond at Sinestra and Kroof. "What will it take you to be grateful?" he stormed. "Mati has proven his worth many times, and you still doubt him. We cannot know what he risked to save Pritin's kits. He is leading us on this journey not on a whim but to save all your skins. Have you no shame?"

Sinestra lowered her head. "But sir, can you be quite sure that he is not, perhaps without intent, the cause of our recent woes? We had few worries before he came to the market-place. That is a fact that none can deny. Trouble stalks the catling. We have all seen it."

Mati closed his eyes. He felt Fiåney tugging at him. Come, Mati, it seemed to beckon – come to a land where you are wanted, accepted, understood.

Pangur's eyes flashed with anger. He pushed past Domino, Trillion and Torko and rounded on Sinestra. Panicked, she cowered, fur sleeked down, ears pressed flat.

"The world is changing!" hissed the chief, standing over her. "Can't you feel it? Mati is not the cause. He is the solution. You are a fool, just like your son! You wish only to divide; to undermine. I won't tolerate this talk any longer – already it has endured too long. Mati saved us from the emptiness, he must be shielded at all costs. He is our friend, a Tygrine, a lord. Our duty is to protect him. Do you understand?"

The chief's loyalty touched Mati deeply. Pangur is all

that I wish I could be, the catling thought – he is brave, confident and honourable. He knows who he is.

Mati opened his eyes. The rain was growing stronger. It clung to his russet fur, rolling off his whiskers. He blinked. For an instant he saw smoke rising from the damp ground, heard a hiss and crackle of flames. The Harakar was close. It was calling him.

Sinestra was staring blankly ahead. He caught a flicker in her dark eyes, felt a tremor of pain. She was thinking of Binjax. Pangur had mentioned her son, and now with some primitive intuition the queen had sensed something of his essence, had awakened to an unutterable dread.

Mati was too absorbed in his own concerns to dwell on Binjax, too distracted by his nagging guilt. I must leave the others as soon as I can, he thought. I must get away. Pangur should not be forced to constantly defend me. Sinestra is right – what have I bought my friends but danger? And now Jess is here too, at risk. The Harakar is in my blood – I stayed there too long. It will never let me go.

He shivered, aware of the faint beating of his own heart. He heard distant barking, although the source was far away. And something else – another rhythm – had the drumming returned, rising from the ground? But hadn't that been Jess?

He glanced at her and she blinked back at him. He felt himself reaching beyond fear and doubt to the world that lingered within her eyes. Against the sombre sky they seemed bright beyond imagining.

134

* * *

For several nights the cats slunk beside fields, weaving between the grasses. The hunters caught rodents while the others took what comfort they could in empty sheds and occasional barns. Drizzle still tumbled mournfully, darkening the sky. It was almost as though the sun had been extinguished, leaving only twilight and darkness.

Cold and tired, the cats slid beneath an abandoned tractor and washed their mottled coats. Awakened to the dangers around them, Pangur put Torko and Arabella on watch while the others slept. Mati curled between Sparrow and Jess and quickly sank into sleep. He dreamt about his kittenhood on the banks of a river, and of his mother, the Tygrine Queen. He heard the rustle of reeds along the bank, and the thick stalks of papyrus flowers casting patterns on the muddy water.

The rain pattered lightly against the tractor and slid along its rusty frame. A droplet escaped to land on Mati's nose. He licked it absently and returned to his reverie. Something had changed – he saw the land of his dream stretch out before him, yet he was no longer part of it. He stood along its dark borders, a stranger.

"Mati?"

He spun round. The voice had emerged from the gloom of the dream-wake. His second self tensed, preparing to fight or flee. A small cat sat in front of him.

"I have sought you in the physical realm but failed to find

135

you. Now I turn to you in Fiåney. Is it, indeed, young Mati?" she said.

"Who wants to know?" He was wary of strangers along the dream-wake's dark boundaries.

"Perhaps you do not remember me?" the small cat asked, her voice trembling with weariness. "My name is Etheleldra." With these words, she came into sharper focus. Mati saw her thinning white fur, her small, low ears; her blind old eyes.

"The cat of the oak," he mumbled in surprise. "The shalian who talks to spirits... You led me into Fiåney, that very first time... You took me to meet the spirit Bayo! He has helped me since, more than once!" Mati spoke with sudden enthusiasm.

"I am glad of it, young cat. Bayo remains true to the cause. Others turn to *him* – you know of whom I speak – he is recruiting allies among the spirits. There are few left now to trust. I urge you to be wary – be wary of everyone."

Mati shuddered, recalling the Cat Lord of the Sa Mau. He pushed the thought away. He was excited to be in the shalian's presence, barely marking her words. "But did you say that you've been looking for me?" he asked. "I've searched for you so many times. For your hollow oak. I have so many questions for you! I've seen terrible things in Fiåney... Where did you go?"

"My time in the physical realm is passing, Mati," the old cat sighed. "I struggle now to realize a presence in that world. Between the two realms, I hover – at the boundaries of sleep, I grow thin. I wish to see you to maturity. I long to know you will be safe. And there are matters I must share with you." Her nose wrinkled. "I wanted to tell you that the air is salty where you are going. Seek water. Run to the sea..."

"The sea?" echoed Mati. He didn't know what else to say. He was aware that the shalian was a friend to the Tygrine; a force for good. Still, he felt uneasy in her presence – scared of the white-eyed cat. "Why the sea?" he asked.

Etheleldra's voice dropped to a whisper. "I have smelled the salty water. So many journeys... I know of your entry into the Harakar."

Mati glanced nervously over his shoulder at hearing this word. No sign remained of the riverbank and long reeds – darkness surrounded him. "What do you know about it?" He hadn't meant to sound suspicious.

"More than you do, catling. It is the chaos land that existed before the Creators forged the earth."

"*His* place."

"No, Mati. Bayo spoke, yet you hardly heeded what he told you." Light shifted about the shalian in leisurely swirls. Mati saw her frown and look away with blind eyes.

"Yes, Bayo helped me but I can't remember much of that now... I was chasing the hawks."

"Try to recall what you can. The pillars – remember the pillars."

"Instinct, judgement and spirit," Mati recited.

"They are not just words." There was a disapproving edge to the shalian's voice. "The pillars are of greatest value in times of crisis. Do not turn your back on them." Mati could hardly hear the old cat and he took a step towards her. She continued. "The Harakar is not *his* place, although he claims it as his own. We should not speak of such things here, at the Borderlands of Fiåney. Someone may be listening..."

A twist of scarlet light glanced through the swirls and Mati shuddered. He tried to remember what Bayo had told him on that terrible journey into the Harakar. "It is the darkland ... the realm beyond the first dark gate."

Etheleldra's ear twitched and her face jerked forward, like a bird. "Yes ... yes, that is good, Mati. The first gate. Few dare enter. It is not like the Borderlands that lie so close to the edge of dreams, so thinly between wakefulness and sleep: the walls of the Harakar are rigid and barbed. It is a prison, a fortress that captures the second self and keeps it in its grip. It is almost impossible to escape."

"I did," Mati pointed out.

The shalian nodded. "You were lucky, for only the Suzerain and his servants have mastered the ability. But it is said that the walls of the Harakar grow thin for mere moments when a physical presence releases their spirit to that realm, or if that spirit returns to its body."

"What are you saying?" asked Mati.

Etheleldra tried to explain. "When a creature that still has

138

a first self – a body, that is – allows its second self to enter the Harakar, the power of its entry forces the walls of the Harakar to fade. Not for long, though, they soon reappear and harden again, in less than the blink of an eye. The same thing happens when the spirit tries to leave."

"You mean that a temporary path, or entrance, opens between the worlds of the first and second self?"

The shalian nodded approvingly. "That is exactly what I mean. Amid the panic of the hawks, desperate to return to the physical realm, you stumbled on an exit."

"I didn't try to get out – I just—"

"Perhaps that is the secret, then. Who can say? Gates to two other lands remain, Sienta and Ra'ha. They will appear to be more yielding, will not seek to trap you by the thickness of their walls, will not use bars or cages that the eye can see. They may seem more inviting, but be wary. These lands mirror the travails of Te Bubas, you understand? The difficult path that was trodden by the very first cat who walked this earth. You must be prepared."

Nothing could be worse than the Harakar, thought Mati. What more had he to fear?

"What comes after the third gate? Is there a fourth?" he asked.

The shalian sucked in her breath. "A fourth? No. There is nothing beyond the third gate. There is only eternity."

"Eternity? But what *is* eternity?" Mati pressed.

The old cat snapped impatiently: "You ask too many

questions! You might have asked me 'what is blue?' Indeed! It is as I said – there is nothing, just endless space and silence."

Mati's fur tingled.

"Do not think of it," said Etheleldra. "I find you lingering here, at the Borderlands, fretting about eternity, awash with questions. I do not waste my time worrying about such things – I worry about you! I know that you have ventured deep along the dream-wake's corridors."

"I've tried to stay away from this place," said Mati, "really I have, because of what I've seen here – the first great battle – is it real? Oh, I know I ask too many questions, Lady Shalian. But believe me, I don't want to stay here, not in the Borderlands or anywhere else in Fiåney! I'll avoid it till I know it's safe, I'll—"

Etheleldra spoke over him testily. "You cannot avoid Fiåney, young cat, it is in your blood. It will call to you. It will find you. You will not be able to resist – and neither should you. For you will need it before the end."

I don't need Fiåney, thought Mati with a shiver. I don't *need* this!

The shalian's ear twitched. "Do not mock Fiåney. Your greatest challenges are yet to come, and you shall depend upon the good grace of those spirits that dare to speak your name. Is it cruelty and hatred that can break your will – or is it love?"

"*Love?*" Mati said the word with surprise. He had no time to think of love. He heard a gush of water and turned to see

140

that the river of his youth had reappeared and was drifting through a nearby dream. He took a step towards it, paused and looked back into Fiåney. The shalian had disappeared.

The Fading Oak

Deep in his chamber, the Suzerain was thinking about Lamet. His senses explored the night for her, but he failed to detect her in the network of streets that encircled the palace. She was out there, somewhere, beyond the reaches of his domain. A cat with brilliant instincts – she might have been a boon sent by Fiåney. But Lamet was reckless, bad at taking orders, slow to reveal her true self. Lost, for now, beyond his powers and designs. Yet the Cat Lord sensed that she still had a part to play in their battle, a role he could not understand. Was she faithful? Would she do what was right, in the end?

"One Law," he murmured, closing his eyes as the high priests circled him, bowing their heads. "One Law for all cat-kind." Irritably, he wondered at how long it was taking for the Three from Fiåney to find the Tygrine. He reproached himself. "I should have waited for a full moon before calling them out." The monster that had exploded from the dream-wake had been damaged from its journey. Fused into one body it moved more slowly than the Suzerain had hoped. If he had waited another day... But no, he would not question what he had done. Great Spirit Alia had allowed it – that was enough. Be they separated or united, the Three would draw energy from the moon. While it waxed and waned, they would quietly approach – when it grew full, they would pounce.

The Suzerain's brow creased as he thought of the Tygrine. That foreign shalian, Etheleldra, had tried to aid the catling and she would pay for it. Did she not know that the walls of Fiåney were thin, particularly at the Borderlands – that her conversation with the Tygrine might be overheard, would be promptly reported to agents of the Sa Mau?

Foolish old cat, thought the Suzerain. No, that was not right. Shalians were many things but they were rarely foolish. She must have been desperate to confer with the Tygrine in the Borderlands. Perhaps she was already too weak to travel deep into the dream-wake's corridors. The thought pleased the Suzerain.

He considered shalians and their role in the feline hier-archy. They were mystics – cats of special powers, with a gift of wisdom and the rare ability to commune with spir-its. They could have been a force for justice and truth. Yet Ipanel and Etheleldra had sought to betray the interests of

Sa. Both had shown worrying sympathies with the Tygrine aggressor. The Suzerain's old teacher had paid the ultimate price for his lapse in loyalty, and Great Spirit Alia would see to the other shalian. "There will be no more mystics in my new order," hissed the Cat Lord. "What is wisdom, when it can be used to question the One Law? When it can corrupt innocence? When it is employed for treachery?"

His eyes opened, falling on one of the high priests, who quailed and bowed, forehead lowered to the ground. "Sire?" uttered the priest. The others continued to circle the chamber, chanting.

"Call the Commander in Chief," said the Suzerain. "Call him now!"

"Yes, Your Most Excellent Majesty," murmured the priest before hurrying out of the chamber.

The Cat Lord was pleased with himself. He had just decided on a new decree: all shalians would be rounded up and disposed of, including the three who remained in court. This was no time for compassion. Shalians were among the few who could pass messages to the spirits. In the great war of the cats, they would be able to distort the Suzerain's words – how could they be trusted?

The Suzerain relaxed. Soon his domain would be endless. Soon there would be nowhere to hide. Already there were creatures in his thrall far beyond its boundaries. There had been the hawks, of course. The hawks had failed to catch the Tygrine ... the hawks had been slain. But there were others. Some of these alliances left the Cat Lord with a sense of discomfort. It would be better to avoid mingling with these creatures, many of whom were a cat's traditional enemies. No matter, he concluded: there were times when uneasy friendships needed to be made for the greater good – particularly if these creatures were prepared to battle the Tygrine. "My enemy's enemy is my friend," rasped the Suzerain. "We shall use them, while we need them... One empire, free from the curse of the Tygrine cat!" His mouth curled back to reveal his fangs.

Thousands of miles away, on a farm at the edge of a distant city, the dogs began to bark.

Etheleldra of the Oak stumbled against the deepening mist that clung to the halls of the dream-wake. She called to Mati with a cracking miaow, scared that an enemy might hear her but fearful at her weakening grip on the spirit realm – she still had so much to tell him. He had changed since their first encounter – yes, she reflected, he had certainly changed. She could scarcely see him of course, now that her sight had failed, but her other faculties were sharp. She sensed his confusion alongside a curious new confidence in Fiåney; she worried at his enduring desire to deny his own destiny. For a cat untutored in the ways of the dream-wake, Mati impressed the shalian. It was clear that he could enter Fiåney's halls at will with scarcely any effort, that he traversed the passageways between dreams as another cat might balance on a garden fence. But was he ready? How could he be?

She turned around sharply, sensing a change in the air.

"Mati?" she miaowed.

The voice that replied was thick and unyielding. "Wrong, old shalian."

"Great Spirit Alia..."

The air before Etheleldra quivered. She swallowed, her throat as dry as sand. The Suzerain's favourite spirit rose in front her, and she knew that she was helpless in the face of such power. She did not beg Alia to spare her — there would be no point. She did not say anything. She simply crouched down against the dream-wake's floor. Resting her head against her paws, she shut her gauzy eyes for the final time.

Watching unseen from the borders of a dream, the spirit Obelghast winced and fled.

A dog walker was the last to lay eyes on the shalian's first self. Hunched in his raincoat and wielding an umbrella against dusk's spattering of rain, he tugged at his collie's lead. At the centre of the park at Cressida Lock, the dog stood transfixed.

"Come on," said the man. "Come on, girl, too cold to be hanging about." He gave its lead a tug but stopped as a faint outline of a cat became visible at his feet. The collie whined and jumped back, smacking into the man's legs

146

and scrambling past them. Straining at the lead, it buried its head in its paws and whimpered. The man stepped away too but he did not turn, and so it was that he saw for a moment, encasing the gossamer outline of the cat, the lofty shape of an oak tree. With his left hand he gripped the collie's lead. His right rose to his eyes, which he rubbed in disbelief. Then it was gone – the shadowy oak – and so too was the small white cat who had, for just a moment, appeared at its heart.

The Night Stalkers

Mati awoke with a start. He thought he had felt a muffled thud against his paws, and heard the faintest sigh sink beneath the falling rain. The day had passed without sunshine – lost to curls of mist and constant drizzle. Now it was almost night once more. As his eyes adjusted to the darkness, he saw Jess and the ferals curled closely around him. Peering below the edge of the abandoned tractor, Arabella turned and blinked at him. Torko was sitting by her side, looking out across the fields.

Mati spotted a lone figure of a cat among tall grasses. It was Pangur, the chief of the Cressida Cats – or at least of the few who had joined them on the journey. Above the chief, the moon hid amid a lattice of clouds, giving the evening sky an unearthly glow.

Mati's ears flicked back. They were all there: Jess,

Domino, Sparrow and the others – all the cats he cared about. And yet he had a nagging sense that something was missing; a premonition of loss. He trod lightly between the sleeping ferals and out into the open where the chief sat in the rain. "Mr Pangur?"

The tomcat turned. His stern face softened when he saw the catling. "You should be sleeping – you most of all."

"You too?" Mati ventured.

"I was thinking." Pangur gazed across the dark fields. "The cats cannot keep going like this. I know you are worried, that you wish to advance. I have supported you, Mati, although it has won me scant popularity. The cats ... they're exhausted. The hawks that took the kits are dead. What else is it you fear?"

Mati paused. "We can find somewhere soon – a new territory," he said carefully. "Perhaps in a day or two. Maybe even tomorrow."

Pangur frowned. "Tomorrow? But you have said, all along..." The chief turned his fierce eyes on Mati. "Can we really just stop, and start anew? Won't it catch up with us?" He watched the catling a moment. "Mati, are you quite sure that we are still being pursued? You wouldn't have us risk our lives in these miserable conditions for – what? No more than a hunch?" Ears back, Pangur searched Mati's face. "Hasn't the time come for answers, young cat? Are we still being followed?"

Mati lowered his head and shut his eyes. He tried to

feel the drumming of paws through the ground but the soil was damp, confiding nothing. "I don't know," he answered honestly.

"You don't *know*?" Pangur's voice was sharp. "What do you mean, you don't know?"

Mati swallowed. "It's this weather. Everything's muffled. My instincts ... it's impossible to tell..."

Pangur was still, absorbing what Mati had told him. When he spoke again there was a steely edge to his voice. "I need you to be frank with me. Think carefully. When was the last time you felt we were being followed?"

Mati couldn't meet his eye. "The night of the hawks," he admitted weakly. "But—"

"You mean to say that the disaster has happened – has been averted – that you have known of no further risk since? But you have let us walk on for days in the rain."

"I cannot feel the presence of the shadow ... but I sense it. Somehow I sense it."

"You *sense* it?" Pangur's eyes narrowed to tiny slits. "As you sensed it at Cressida Lock?"

"Yes," Mati murmured. He suddenly felt very small, as if he was shrinking, while Pangur grew large and menacing.

"We left Cressida Lock because Sparrow was poisoned – because the cats believed that this was linked to your warnings, that evil was at work. But can you be sure of that? Can you be certain that the poison wasn't left by hinds for their own ends? What if it had nothing to do with the danger of which you speak? I have been wondering about this and it doesn't make sense to me. Poison left by cats? It is a hind invention, is it not? A symptom of their own particular cruelty."

Mati swallowed. Pangur was right – poison was distinctly un-catlike. All of a sudden it seemed obvious that the incident with Sparrow had nothing to do with the Suzerain, the Harakar or anything else. Yet Pangur and the others who had left Cressida Lock with Mati had done so as a result of the poisoning, believing that it was only the beginning – that danger was coming to the market-place. Had it all been a terrible mistake?

Pangur caught the doubt on Mati's face. Seething, he turned away. "I trusted you," he uttered. "I trusted you entirely."

"I'm sorry… Maybe – maybe it's true that the poison was left by hinds. But that's reason enough to leave, isn't it? I mean, if the hinds are starting to poison the market cats…" Mati paused. It was more than that. He tried again. "Mr Pangur, you have to believe me – there *was* something approaching the market-place. I think there really was."

"You 'think'," hissed Pangur. "You *'think'* too much." Without looking back, he stalked away into the darkness.

The chief gruffly relieved Arabella and Torko of their duties, appointing Domino and Ria to keep watch. He disappeared again into nearby fields, his damp coat gleaming. Mati settled between Sparrow and Jess and shut his eyes. He listened to the braying wind and the pitter-patter of rain-drops against the rusty tractor.

Pangur is right, he thought dismally. I have no reason to believe that the poison Sparrow ate was anything to do with the Sa Mau. It could easily have been left by hinds. Cats fight with teeth and claws; cats stalk in darkness and trap their prey. They do not deal in poison.

The weight of this realization dawned upon Mati. Had he really led the company away from their homes for noth-ing? Maybe the sense of pursuit he had felt was simply his friend Jess trying to catch up with them. Yet a dark chill had touched him at the sound of the drumming paws. And what of the hawks of the Harakar?

"Do you miss Binjax?" whispered Domino, washing a black-and-white tail.

Mati was surprised at this question before realizing that it wasn't directed at him.

"A bit," admitted Ria. "I wish he'd come with us. He's so stubborn. But it isn't the same without him..." She lowered her head.

"I bet he's loving it though, being a chief," said Domino, trying to lighten the mood. "I reckon he's bossing everyone around, getting them to treat him like a king!"

Ria nodded. "Yes," she said, uncertainly. "But I sense ... I feel..." The silver tabby didn't finish her sentence. Something was creeping through the distant gloom. "What's that?" she hissed.

152

Domino's back arched. "An oolf!" He squinted.

"It's pretty far away," said Ria. "It can't have spotted us."

"Should we wake the others?"

The catlings watched as the dog seemed to hesitate, sniffing the air, before veering away into the darkness.

"It's gone," Ria sighed, her tail relaxing behind her. She paused. "I don't like it out here. Wish we were back at Cressida Lock."

"Me too," admitted Domino.

He has made a great show of approving of this journey, pretending to enjoy it for my sake, thought Mati. But in his heart he longs for the market-place. I have taken him – all of them – away from their homes. I could have been wrong about the poison, about everything. Pangur has lost faith in me. How can I blame him?

Warmth gathered at the base of Mati's paws and he breathed deeply. It was the dream-wake, beckoning to him. He didn't want to fight it any more. Hadn't the shalian told him that in any event he couldn't – that he would be unable to resist Fiåney? His body relaxed against the grass, while his second self drifted effortlessly into the land of spirits.

That all-encompassing veil of darkness wrapped itself around him, drawing him deeper, deeper into the vaults of the dream-wake. For moments that could have been the blinking of an eye or the passage of seasons, Mati felt himself borne on a lazy current. He might have drifted this way for ever, in total silence and tranquillity, but chance, fate or a faceless design led him to an indigo light, and the junction he had visited before.

Branching from the junction were three passageways. Smoke billowed from the passage to his right. Mati knew that it led to the Harakar – the land beyond the first gate. With a fresh gust of smoke, an unearthly screech escaped the Harakar, causing the fur to rise along Mati's neck. He turned towards the middle passage. The air around him seemed to slow as he approached it and silence enclosed him once more. He lifted a russet paw, meaning to advance towards the passage. It stretched before him, and far away in the distance danced a pale yellow haze. Mati pushed on towards it, struggling against the thick, silent air.

He continued like this, his paws treading along the middle passage, without any sense of distance or time. The yellow haze glinted out of reach, scarcely growing, still unimaginably far away. A vague memory played on Mati as he padded towards the light, a warning from Etheleldra not to abandon his body too long – not to stray too deep.

Soon, thought Mati. Just a little further...

The yellow sky deepened to orange and finally to red. He walked for what felt like an age, finding it increasingly hard to lift his paws. His body hardly seemed to be moving at all, but at the end of the passage he saw a sandy hilltop advance gradually towards him. Rocks were gathered there in a small mound. Overhead the sky was crimson, frozen

154

without movement or sound. Mati had the feeling that he had been to this place many times before – not only in Fiåney but in this and perhaps even previous lives.

He gazed at the hill longingly. More than anything, he wanted to be up there, amid the rock mound. Instead, he stood in a vast, sandy valley. It was the same valley where the first great battle had taken place between the armies of the Tygrine and the Sa. No evidence remained of its violent past, except perhaps the crimson sky.

Mati stood still. Nearby, he could sense the presence of water, the faintest murmur of a listless river. He listened closer. Someone was coming – approaching from the hilltop overlooking the valley. He lifted his head gradually – for everything moved slowly in this place – and there he saw the silhouette of a cat. Against the scarlet sky he could scarcely make out her russet coat, dappled back or the strange white marking along her spine. He couldn't see her golden eyes that tilted up at the corners between wide spaced ears. But he knew it was Te Bubas – the first cat – and his jaw fell in awe.

Ria licked a tabby paw, sweeping it over her face and ears. Domino was by her side but he had drifted off to sleep and she had let him, resolving to wake him if anything seemed suspicious. The evening had dragged into night and the drizzle had finally finished, but the air was damp, mist curling round the tractor, underneath which the ferals slept. Ria felt a need to wash herself, to rid her fur of a clinging chill. Try as she might, she could not shake off the sadness that hung on her coat. The unspeakable fear that something had happened to her brother Binjax.

Ria froze, paw suspended above her head. She had smelled something unpleasant on the night air – something *unclean*. She heard a scuffling sound just beyond the tractor. Her eyes narrowed and her fur swelled. Heart racing, paw still held above her face, too scared to move, she counted: one … two … no, more, more like three, or four … *six?*

"Domino!" she hissed, finding her voice. "Oolfs … lots of oolfs!"

His eyes flew open and rising he saw that the dark shapes of dogs were moving towards them. He raised the alarm with an ear-piercing cry.

Several beasts were closing in on them. "A pack of oolfs!" cried Domino.

The ferals sprang to life, at once alert. The dogs were closing in, snarling and barking, drool heavy on gummy mouths. Pangur appeared from just beyond the tractor, on the far side of the dogs, his fur glossy in the damp air. Instantly he was in control. "Down to the river, to the brambles!" he ordered. "Deep in as you can. Up any passing trees. *Go!*"

The ferals bolted past Pangur, who stood his ground, waiting for the last to leave. He turned sharply. Jess was pawing at a mound of fur, her bell tinkling frantically. "It's

Mati!" she miaowed: "I can't wake him!"

A clamour exploded around the catling, the mewling of Jess, the frenzied barking. But deep within Fiâney, silence surrounded him.

The dogs had arrived, but Mati heard nothing.

Sienta

A faint glow hovered around Te Bubas, a glimmer of honeyed light.

Her voice came to Mati, was all around him in Fiåney first – as though it had no relation to the first cat on the distant hilltop:

"Before time, there was the Harakar – the turbulent land of fire and water. Then came Sienta, a place of order, of balance. The Creators frowned at the Harakar's chaos, at its unbidden cruelty and despair. They commanded the Harakar into exile – but it did not perish. It only lay in wait, hiding behind the first gate, furious as the earliest implacable sea, lashing against the stability of our world. Its moon it left over our sky, a final act of defiance – a moon that longed for the return of chaos, that searches for the fragility of the sun's order when darkness falls, like the eye of the night."

The queen on the hilltop moved so close to the steep edge that Mati held his breath.

She spoke again. "The earth was forged by the will of the Creators. The same will that made me."

Instead of backing away, the queen leapt, her limbs impossibly long and agile as she flew over the cliff-face, as though in slow motion. The sky behind her flickered before blossoming into the shape of the first cat, an echo of the queen who was still leaping, timelessly, from the hilltop down to the valley. The floating image of Te Bubas wept, and from her tears sprang two kittens.

"To have is to lose, the earth was soon to learn. And so I too learned."

The figure of the first cat in the distance blinked, and the kittens melted into the sand. With them, the image faded once more into a blood-red sky and the pouncing cat finally landed in the valley a short distance from Mati. Her golden eyes were wide open, glowing with energy. This time the voice escaped her throat, rather than rising from the land around him:

"Child, are you here?" she purred. "Follow me."

Mati longed to run to this cat, to bury his face in the nape of her neck, but his legs refused to move. He watched with alarm as Te Bubas backed away, prancing out into the desert, far into the valley. In an instant she was a distant silhouette.

Please come back, Mati pleaded wordlessly. The first

cat seemed to pause, as though reading his thoughts. She half turned her head, and he wondered for a moment if she would return to him. Instead, Mati saw with surprise that another cat was walking alone through the sandy valley, appearing in the distance – a beautiful catling with long legs and spots across her back. She hurried towards the first cat with a freedom of movement that Mati did not share: a friend of Fiåney, at ease in this quiet place.

Mati watched as Te Bubas lowered her face to the catling, licking her brow adoringly. Standing some distance away, to the south of the valley, he felt like an intruder. He knew that he should leave, yet he lingered. Te Bubas did not turn again, but at that moment the spotted catling lifted her head and gazed at Mati, as if noticing him for the first time. As their eyes met he felt a flash of lightning, a thrill of delight that was oddly accompanied by fear. Mati stared at the stranger in wonder. He noticed with surprise that one of her eyes was green, the other golden. The young queen stared back, her expression unreadable. Then she looked away and sprang off again, Te Bubas at her side. Mati watched their retreating forms until they were specks on the horizon, and then he was quite alone. He lifted a front paw and found that he could move once more, but the queens were gone – too far within the space called Sienta for Mati ever to find them.

He wondered at the catling with the spotted back and remarkable eyes. Who was she? In the silence of Sienta, a

160

single word seemed to rise from the sand: *"Lamet."*

With a sense of unutterable sorrow, Mati retreated from the world of the Creators, backed towards the junction of the three passageways. There he paused in the indigo light, wondering how he would ever find Te Bubas again, and the beautiful queen who had run with her beyond his reach. Then a gust of smoke escaped from the Harakar, and with it Mati felt the drumming of paws drawing closer. Not the light, fluid steps of the cats of Sienta but something jagged, fractured... Over it, the clamour of baying dogs chilled his blood.

Life flooded back to Mati's legs, to his paws, and weakly he opened his eyes. The clashing barks rang in his ears as gusts of putrid breath caught in his throat. It took a moment for the shapes of the dogs to come into focus, looming over him with dripping jowls. He was alone beneath the rusty tractor – the other cats had disappeared. No. Someone was just behind him, pawing him, urging him to get up. It was Jess.

One of the dogs seemed to be the leader, a thickly-furred beast with a wolfish snout. Snarling, it lowered itself by the edge of the tractor, shoving its furry muzzle underneath. Its mouth was open, revealing juicy pink gums and fangs oozing with spit. Its mouth widened into a fiendish grin, the snarl growing, as the other dogs closed in. One reached beneath the tractor with a clumsy paw. Mati gaped, dazed.

161

In a moment they would seize him, would make their hideous sport of him.

A yowl cut through the night air. Heads snapped back in unison. Pangur stood a few paces away, daring them to chase him. His fur was puffed up and he appeared twice his size. The dogs barked wildly and Pangur backed away, almost in slow motion. "To the brambles," he hissed, addressing Jess and Mati though his eyes never left the wolfish dog.

Feeling flooded back to Mati's limbs and awkwardly he rose to his paws. His legs trembled. What had happened to him?

"Come on!" urged Jess. He met her eye and she blinked, turned and scrambled out from under the tractor. He followed her more slowly, his bones rigid and unyielding, as if he had aged on his last trip to Fiåney – as though he was ancient.

The dogs were still barking at Pangur, oblivious of the catlings' escape from the tractor. Already Jess was halfway to the bramble bush with Mati lagging behind her before a stumpy mongrel at the back of the group caught the movement from the corner of his eye. He broke from the pack with a burst of excited yaps, scurrying after the catlings. The other dogs shot round and suddenly everyone was running; the catlings in a straight line to the bramble bush; Pangur sprinting at an angle to a distant tree; the dogs divided in a fever of excitement.

Mati was gripped with dread. He had heard how dogs

dispatched their quarry. They would lock their huge jaws around its neck, shaking frantically until it snapped, or physically tear it limb from limb. Banishing these thoughts, Mati tore after Jess. He felt light-headed and he staggered as he ran, blinking against the rain. Jess had shot towards the bramble bush and was already nosing her way inside, but he was lagging. Risking a glance over his shoulder, he saw that the small dog was gaining on him, yapping at his tail.

With a surge of energy Mati drove himself forward, seeing the brambles rise overhead with their network of spindly branches. He scrambled beneath them, eyes clamped shut, heedless of the thorns that nicked his fur.

"Thank goodness!" cried Domino. "You had us worried sick."

Mati opened his eyes. The voice had floated from deep within the brambles and he could not make out his friend beyond the fortress of branches.

"Come in further," urged Jess's voice. "Oolfs won't get far here, but they'll try to... Just come in further!"

Mati sighed, pushing deeper. A branch caught against his shoulder and he winced. Suddenly, pressure clamped around his back paw and pain darted up his leg. The barking behind him was manic. One of the dogs was snapping at his leg and had managed a tentative hold. It was trying to drag him out of the bush. The other dogs were out there, wild on the cat's fear. Breathlessly, Mati struggled, freeing himself from the dog and diving through the brambles until he reached Jess and the ferals. They were gathered together, almost on top of each other, in an opening at the heart of the bush. He collapsed against Sparrow, panting as the older cat washed his fur protectively.

Sparrow's good eye widened. "You're hurt!"

"It's nothing." One of Mati's back legs throbbed vaguely and he licked it, tasting his own blood. It didn't hurt too much – not yet. But the pain was on its way, clustering at the edges of Mati's senses.

Jess was watching him. "What happened to you? I couldn't wake you!"

Mati lowered his face. "I don't know," he mumbled. The land of the Creators seemed hopelessly out of reach – the gentle glance of Te Bubas now less than the faintest memory. Instead he looked up and saw his friend's eyes still gazing at him. "Did you see where Pangur got to?"

Mati was silent. The chief had bolted in a different direction, drawing the dogs behind him, distracting them from Mati. He hadn't returned.

Beyond the bramble bush, the dogs still barked, pawing at the branches excitedly. One whined in frustration but none would cross the thorny barricade. They snarled and yapped until the moon set beyond the clouds. Finally, they lost interest and padded away into surrounding fields. Still there was no sign of Pangur.

* * *

Few slept in the hours until dawn. The rain had finally ceased and the sun hung over the sky once more, peeping through the clouds.

Mati leaned against Sparrow's back, awkwardly lifting his sore leg and washing it as best he could. The bite stung but he had to clean it – dogs were known to be dirty animals. His ears pricked up. Someone was outside the bramble bush, nosing his way in. Mati tensed. The scent of the Cressida chief wafted towards him before the glossy black face appeared.

Mati breathed a sigh of relief. He hadn't realized till that moment how tense he had been, how anxious he was to know that Pangur was safe.

He distracted the oolfs to save me, thought Mati. He swallowed. "I thought..."

Pangur's eyes glittered. "What? That I'm no match for a few oolfs?" He stared a moment. Then he pirruped. "Come, cats – time to leave this place."

With careful steps, they followed their chief out of the bramble bush.

The ferals stalked uphill again, at the borders of fields where harvested corn was stacked in golden bales. Pangur was in the lead with Trillion at his side. At the end of the line trailed Mati, limping slightly and struggling to keep up.

"Are you feeling all right?" asked Jess, just ahead of him.

Mati nodded, focusing his attention on setting one paw ahead of another.

165

"Last night I couldn't wake you," she went on. "You know that, don't you? That the oolfs came, and everyone ran, but you slept through it."

The Tygrine lowered his head. I wasn't asleep, he thought. I was deep in Fiåney. *Too deep.*

Mati remembered something that the shalian, Etheleldra, had told him at their first meeting: "A mortal cat who ventures into Fiåney must leave their body behind at the gateway to the realms. But the body must not be left for long. To travel too far into that mysterious land – to attempt to leap across seas, to cross continents – could spell doom. A cat could get lost in Fiåney, where only the ever-shifting borders of dreams mark the way. A cat might vanish in the spirit world and never find their way home."

I've been foolish, thought Mati. I knew that I was going further than I had before. But I didn't want to think about it – I just had to keep going.

A word drifted into his head: *Sienta.* Was that the land beyond the second gate? Yes, Mati remembered now, that's what Te Bubas had said. Hadn't Etheleldra also mentioned it? She had told him that there was a third gate too, and another land he had yet to visit.

Sienta was different from the Harakar, opposite to the land of chaos and flames. Sienta was ordered and calm, a place of solitude – Te Bubas's place. He recalled the first cat and he longed for her. He had wanted more than anything to follow her into her silent world, to be accepted by Te

Bubas. But by following her Mati endangered himself, and his friends too. Jess had stayed with his body, his first self... Pangur had distracted the dogs... All these risks to protect me, thought Mati.

He wondered about the arrival of the dogs. How had they found the kin? It was almost as though they knew that the cats were out there – almost as if they'd been sent. *The Suzerain*, thought Mati, his hairs rising. The Suzerain knows that I'm here.

Daisy's Farmyard

The sounds of the city had long since faded. In every direction stretched lonely fields. Once more, the river had retreated behind brambles and spiky hedgerows, before curving away to the west. The cats kept moving, hidden among tall grasses at the verges of fields, without clear purpose or destination. They were all hungry and tired. The eldest like Sparrow felt it the worst and the kittens also struggled to keep pace. At the back limped Mati, throwing nervous glances over his shoulder. He almost bumped into Sparrow, who came to a halt behind the others, looking around, confused.

"What's going on?" asked Mati. He nosed past Sparrow but could hardly see beyond the furry heads and twitching ears of the ferals.

"Not sure, lad," wheezed Sparrow, grateful only that they

had stopped. He sat down heavily and yawned.

The other cats were murmuring among themselves. "Why aren't we moving?" he heard Arabella ask, addressing no one in particular.

"Mati?" called Domino. Wariness tempered his usual confidence. The unexpected appearance of the dogs had affected everyone. Who was to say what was out here among these quiet country fields?

The ferals parted to let Mati pass, each cat watching him curiously. Could this cat be their rescuer, or was he responsible for their misfortunes? Mati stared blankly ahead, recalling what Pangur had said the previous night – that Sparrow's poisoning had been an unrelated coincidence; that the Tygrine had led them to unspeakable danger, and for nothing.

Mati slunk close to the ground. His tail followed deject-edly, brushing against grass. Ahead of him stood Pangur, dark and irascible. The chief's tail twitched as Mati approached. Behind him Mati saw a farm complex, with two large houses, a stable with giant, long-faced animals – "Horses," said Jess authoritatively – and a series of storage barns.

Mati took in the neat front lawn before the houses, a series of apple trees and some cleared flowerbeds. He wasn't sure what else he was supposed to be looking at, so he turned his amber eyes to the chief. Pangur stared at him, saying nothing.

Trillion spoke. "He wants to know if this is a possibility," she said. Mati started. Under Pangur's searching eyes he had almost forgotten that the other cats were there.

Mati cleared his throat. "A possibility?"

"Whether we might stay here ... start a new home. We can't walk any more. Who lives here, Mati? Are there any—" she narrowed her eyes— "any oolfs? Or other cats? We've heard that barns are good for mice. Hinds store grain in them, and the mice come to feed. We'd have rich pickings... But is it safe?"

Mati nodded in understanding. "I'll try to find out," he said quietly. He took a deep breath and shut his eyes. These days he didn't need to think of rhymes or chants to sink into Fiâney. The dream-wake was always there, stalking the edges of his consciousness. Heat crackled through his paws and in a moment his senses were reaching along the driveway to the houses and around the neighbouring barns. The ferals watched, exchanging glances. By now they had learned that when Mati's body froze, his mind wandered – that much went on beyond the grasp of their own senses.

Soon his eyes opened. He blinked dazedly at the ferals, reminding himself where he was. Finding Trillion's face among them, he directed his words to her: "So many mice," he began, to excited murmurs from the ferals. "There are colonies of grey ones all round the barns, and tiny, chestnut mice with long tails in the fields. They have rats too." To this there were growls and crinkled noses from the ferals. "Not in the same numbers, though," Mati said quickly. "The grey mice are definitely the biggest group around. Perhaps they were scared of the rats once ... but they don't seem to be any more. They're bold, entering the barns, the stables, the houses. Safety in numbers."

"How about oolfs?" Trillion prompted and the ferals tensed.

Mati shook his head. "No oolfs. There are the hinds, and those giant, nervous animals that live in the fields. What did you call them, Jess?"

She stepped forward. "Horses."

Mati blinked at her. "They don't seem dangerous, whatever they are."

"Any cats?" asked Trillion.

"Just one. She lives in a barn. I sense she was quite a mouser in her youth, but I doubt that she catches much these days. She is old, her bones brittle. She can hardly see and she can't run fast. She isn't scared of the hinds. There are a small number in each house. I'd say they like her. She's relaxed around them. I think they may even feed her." His eyes drifted to Pangur, who was watching him with a blank expression.

"Where is this old cat?" Pangur asked.

"The nearer barn," replied Mati.

"Take me," said Trillion. She followed Mati up the driveway as the other cats watched.

After a moment, Mati turned. Pangur wasn't coming with them. He shot Trillion a quizzical look but Domino's mother did not meet his eye.

They hurried along the side of one of the farmhouses. Mati noticed an empty dish, next to a bowl of water. He licked his muzzle.

Trillion sniffed the dish. "They're feeding her," she agreed.

The old cat was dozing on a low beam inside one of the barns and didn't hear Mati and Trillion as they slid between a couple of loose slats. Her rumpled fur was mostly grey with a few white patches, including a splodge on her chin. She wore no collar round her neck, nothing to indicate that she owned humans. Perhaps she is more like a feral, thought Mati, living among hinds but not granting socage, not entering their homes.

Trillion cleared her throat loudly and the old cat jumped, fur rising. "Who are you?" she hissed.

"I am Trillion, Mistress of Hunts. This is Mati, Lord of the Tygrine Cats. We come in friendship."

Mati noticed that she dropped the *pirrups* and the lofty salutations — the "Courageous" and "Sagacious" that normally preceded correct titles. He remembered that these were traditions of the market cats — perhaps she wanted to avoid confusion, or to sound more humble.

The old cat frowned, standing on the beam. Her back

172

legs trembled. "Why are you here?"

Trillion sat, indicating with a jerk of the head that Mati should do the same. "Honourable stranger," here she pir-ruped, "we have travelled a great distance. We come from far away, along a river – a noisy place filled with hinds. We wish permission for an audience with you." She lowered her face and waited.

The old cat watched them. "Very well," she replied. "But you will have to speak up. My ears are not what they were."

"Of course." Trillion cleared her throat. "My name is Trillion of Cressida Lock. The catling is Mati." This time she abandoned formalities altogether. "We do not own hinds, and never have – we are independent. We come from a market-place where for generations our kin has lived alongside hinds in relative peace."

The old cat stared at her.

Trillion continued. "Things have changed. Circum-stances... The hinds left poison. One of our kin was hurt."

The old cat hissed involuntarily. "They tried to kill the cats?"

Mati's ears flicked back. Trillion had been talking to Pangur. She too had concluded that the poison was left by humans. She must have doubted Mati's reasons for leaving Cressida Lock. What did she think of him?

Trillion sighed. "We still cannot believe it or understand. We don't know why they did it. The world is changing..."

Mati stole a glance at the grey-and-white. She was

173

studying Trillion between narrowed eyes. She has seen changes too, he thought. She has known love and loss; she has given birth to kittens and watched as they were taken away; she has learned to trust hinds, but not too much.

"It was no longer safe in the market-place. We had to leave," said Trillion. "We followed the river for many nights. We have just arrived here, tired and hungry. We appeal to your compassion."

The old cat was silent, considering Trillion's words. Mati sensed that this story had touched her. That she knew what it was to be tricked by humans. That she knew what it was to be cast out of her home. "You are all here?" she asked. "The whole kin?"

"Only a few of us left our Territory – the rest of the kin stayed behind. Those who came are waiting in a nearby field."

"What is it you would have me do?"

Trillion held the old cat's gaze. "We wish to settle here, with your good grace. To help you with your hunting tasks. To be accepted by the local hinds. To make a home."

Mati was thinking. Outside he heard the twittering of birds and the distant neigh of horses. He smelled barley, peat and manure: soothing smells that would quickly feel like home. If the cats stayed here he could leave, alone, at twilight, knowing that they had found somewhere safe to rebuild their lives.

"I do not need help with hunting," said the old cat proudly.

Trillion did not contradict her. "We are hungry and tired. There are kits among us. We long to rest."

The old cat watched a long while, unblinking. Then she looked away. "There are kits with you?" She stared across the barn at nothing in particular — nothing that could be seen with the eyes.

"Yes, two young kits."

The old cat blinked. "The hinds call me Daisy. I had another name once — a name my amma gave me. But that was a long time ago."

"What was it?" asked Mati.

It was the first time he had spoken and the old cat started, surprised to hear his voice. Her mouth opened slightly as she took in his golden eyes. She studied his face, his russet fur and large, pointed ears. "I don't remember." Her ear twitched and she turned back to Trillion. "Where is your chief? Why have you not brought him to see me?"

Mati had wondered the same thing. Pangur had stayed on the outskirts of the field with the kin. Why hadn't he come to entreat the old cat? Surely it was his role?

Trillion raised her head, her eyes wide and unblinking. "I am the chief."

While Jess and the ferals followed Trillion to Daisy's barn, Pangur gestured for Mati to stay behind.

"Trillion said…" Mati trailed off under Pangur's stare.

"She is bold, and fair, a fine mouser and a wise thinker. She will be a good chief."

Mati thought this was true. "What about you?" he asked warily.

The black tom's eyes sparkled. "I am going with you."

"Going where?"

"Wherever you lead me. A couple of the others may also come. Domino and Jess, I imagine. I have discussed it with Trillion – she is prepared to let her son go. I have not yet spoken to them. I wanted to tell you first."

Mati stared at Pangur in disbelief. "But you are the leader of the kin."

"What 'kin'? Most remained at Cressida Lock. The rest will be happy with Trillion in charge."

"Mr Pangur…" Mati looked down at his russet paws. "I think you were right about the poison. The hinds must have left it…"

"You may have been wrong about the poison, but the hawks and the dogs were real enough. I have been thinking. Remembering when the spotted cat came, the night I fought my brother. Its kin are still out there, aren't they? Still searching for you?"

Mati nodded, recalling Mithos and the cats of the Sa Mau.

"And you thought you would sneak away, leaving us to set up a new territory?"

Mati raised his head. "How did you guess?"

Pangur's tail swished. "I may not have access to the spirit realm, but I am not a total fool. Once you knew that the others were staying put, and fearing such danger, what else could you do?"

"Yes. I plan to leave alone."

"Now you don't have to. You may need friends on your journey – wherever you are going."

Mati wanted to leap at Pangur, to purr uncontrollably, to bury his face in the tom's black fur. Instead he blinked. "Thank you," he murmured. It didn't seem like enough. He looked out over the distant fields. "Shall we—"

"Not now," said Pangur. He may no longer have been chief, but his voice was thick with authority. "First I must know that the cats have been accepted, that they are safe. And you must rest your leg. We will leave in a few nights."

Mati's hopes sank. Did they have a few nights? He felt no tremor of distant footsteps but he knew that something was out there, that the chase continued. How long would his stalker take to arrive?

"Not now," repeated Pangur. "And don't think of sloping off by yourself. I have read the thought in your eyes. I am watching you. I won't allow it – you serve no one if you are injured and weak."

Mati nodded reluctantly and Pangur began to purr. Satisfied, the black tom started towards Daisy's barn. Mati shot a glance over his shoulder, where birds twittered in

177

hedgerows and sunshine hung over patchwork pastures. What could a short delay hurt? But over the bird song he heard murmurings from Fiåney, spirits troubled with discontent. Whiskers bristling, Mati wondered if he'd made a mistake.

Pangur's Denial

That night the hunters set out to catch as many mice as possible. The tiny creatures were taken by surprise and the pickings were plentiful. Their warm bodies were offered to Daisy in thanks and shared among the ferals, with higher-order cats like Pangur and Trillion taking first pick.

"Those ones look delicious!" said Domino, approaching a separate pile of mice by Trillion's paws.

"Not these," she reproved. "These are for the hinds. We still need more though. Hunting all night – it's the only way. If the plan works, we rest in the morning."

"The hinds?" Domino stared in confusion. "Hinds don't eat mice, do they?"

"An offering. Daisy has told us how they hate the mice, because they eat the wheat and corn from the fields.

Hinds eat that stuff too."

Standing next to Trillion, Daisy blinked her agreement. She had suggested this strategy in order that the local humans would accept the new arrivals. She knew of their frustration at the number of mice and hoped that this cull would impress them.

"Yes, indeed, we must sacrifice these mice, deny our bellies, in the interests of the greater good!" put in Sparrow enthusiastically. "A clever gambit by Daisy – a very clever gambit!"

Domino nodded vaguely. He didn't really understand but the other cats were watching and he didn't want to seem dim.

Trillion presided over the distribution of the mice and the other cats accepted this without question. Pangur had explained that he would leave with Mati, Jess and Domino. Perhaps all the changes of recent days had made the cats more open to the inevitability of surprises. It was clear that the Tygrine's journey was not over, even if their travels had reached an end.

Sparrow had reacted with distress to the news, insisting that he should come too. Pangur was dismissive: the old ginger tom would slow them down. Jess was ready to leave – she had never really fitted in. It was Domino who feared the separation most. He was close to his mother and the other cats.

Sitting at a distance, Mati was troubled. He had eaten a

mouse, chewing on its long thin tail until there was nothing left. A salty flavour remained in his mouth. Again and again his eyes rose to the sky. Through the barn's wooden roof, he could not see the moon but he knew it was there and he shifted uneasily.

He pressed his paws against the ground, willing them to absorb its vibrations. Outside the barn, he sensed the movements of the cats who stalked mice in the cornfield, the light taps of their fleshy paw pads glancing off the earth. He froze a moment longer and waited. With relief, he began to relax. *Wait!* There was that drumming again, closer now but still faint, a light, erratic *thump-thump-thump.*

Mati shot a look across the barn, knowing he would see nothing unusual – that the cause of the drumming was still far away. But how far? It seemed to be speeding up, the trembling beats against the ground growing faster. Was it gaining on the kin? He shut his eyes and he knew – knew with absolute certainty: it was coming, travelling only in the hours of darkness. A creature with its own, mysterious calling; that couldn't be thwarted by distance alone. It was closing on the ferals.

"Now, Mati," instructed a voice in his head. The voice was husky, unfamiliar, and he hesitated, looking around. The cats were absorbed in their meal, crunching contentedly. He looked across at the dark end of the barn. He had already observed an exit there, a narrow gap between the wooden slats. He could be out in a moment and hurrying over the fields. He wouldn't be able to move fast, not with his sore leg, but he would still make progress. By the time the ferals realized he was gone, it would be too late to catch him. This was in direct defiance of Pangur's command, Mati reflected guiltily. He had promised the former chief that he would rest a while, that they would leave together with Jess and Domino. But there were times when even leaders made mistakes, isn't that what the past had taught him?

He remembered Etheleldra's counsel: he had to trust his instincts above all else. The thought of her suddenly made him sad. Would he see the old shalian again? he wondered. With a chill, he suspected the answer but he pushed it away, scared of facing the truth.

Very slowly, Mati rose from his haunches. Pain shot through his injured leg and he paused, waiting for it to subside. Then he backed towards the wall, one step at a time.

It's better this way, he thought. My friends will be safe.

He threw a look at Domino, who was still enjoying the feast. Sparrow was talking to Daisy, telling her all about his kittenhood at Cressida Lock.

"A splendid spot in my romping days!" he purred. "Established by two extraordinary queens, did you know that? Great Founders, *Pirrup*: the Courageous Ladies Wilhelmina and Moullier, Consorts of Freedom. Queens are so much cleverer at these things, that's the truth. Toms get…" Sparrow frowned, his bad eye squinting. "Well, we get a little muddled." He fell silent for a moment, while Daisy

182

watched him expectantly. Then he seemed to remember himself. "You would simply adore Cressida Lock, I am sure, a cat of such evident discernment. Madam, another mouse?"

"Thank you, I shall," replied Daisy as he dropped the limp creature before her. "I have heard about town cats. Out here they are said to be – well, I do not wish to offend – but rather *raffish* characters. I find that this slur is far from the truth."

"Oh, there are some rogues!" exclaimed Sparrow in a scandalized whisper – though not a particularly quiet one. "You would scarcely believe a few of the toms that have passed through the market-place over the years. In fact, there are a couple of questionable distinction who remained there… Let us say they are little missed. But we do our best, we certainly try."

Mati edged towards the gap between the slats. He did not seek out Jess in the group. He could not bear to look at her. She had travelled so far to be with him and he had put her in danger. How would she feel when she discovered he was gone? Would she understand?

His heart quickened as he backed beneath the shadows at the rear of the barn, turning to crawl between the gap. His right paw reached out, curling round the slat, feeling a chill ruffle his fur.

A hiss against his ear made him freeze with terror: "One more step and I'll rip out your throat."

It was Pangur.

* * *

Early the next morning, the farmer and his daughter opened their front door to a mound of dead mice. They glanced at each other in surprise. A crackly miaow awakened them to Daisy's presence and they watched as several other cats appeared behind her.

"What's all this about?" said the farmer.

Daisy miaowed again.

"Look at all these mice!" exclaimed his daughter.

"Seems ol' Daisy's had some help."

"Good job, I'd say."

The farmer grunted. "A bit of a motley crew. Where'd they come from? No farms nearby."

His daughter shrugged. "Maybe someone dumped them." She reached out her hand, beckoning the cats.

"Domino, go over to her," said Trillion.

A young black-and-white approached nervously and brushed the woman's fingertips with his nose. The other cats stood where they were, a few paces behind Daisy, waiting.

"It's like they're expecting something," said the farmer.

"If they're that good at hunting, they'd be an asset, wouldn't they?" The farmer's daughter tickled the black-and-white under the chin. He started to purr obligingly. "Maybe we can keep 'em?"

"I've got enough mouths to feed. Getting the sheep tomorrow."

"But they could feed themselves on the mice. We'd just leave a few nibbles out to make sure they stay. Nothing else seems to help. Poor ol' Daisy's not up to much. Dad, we're overrun and you know it."

"Can't move for rodents. I'd poison the lot if it didn't risk the crops an' livestock."

"But it does, and you can't. The bloke with the traps didn't do much. Cats would be better. Look at this mound. You've got to admit it's impressive, Dad."

The farmer started towards the fields, his daughter following. "It's turning into a ruddy zoo around here," he snorted. "I'm not having them in the house."

Daisy watched them go. "Well, they didn't shoo you away," she said to Domino.

Jess had been listening, standing among the ferals. "I usually understand hinds, but I don't really know what this means."

"I think we just wait now," said Trillion. "We wait and see and we look out for signs of trouble."

The cats withdrew to Daisy's barn and rested after their long night of hunting.

Mid-morning, Trillion followed Daisy out of the barn. Next to Daisy's dish of water were several new plates of dry catfood. Daisy started purring. "I think this means you're staying," the old cat said.

Mati hadn't joined the others in front of the farmer's house.

He hadn't left the barn since Pangur had caught him trying to escape. The former chief was angry that his orders had been ignored. Although neither Pangur nor Mati mentioned the catling's thwarted escape to the ferals, it was clear that an atmosphere clung to them, and the others kept away.

I'm stuck here now, thought Mati, stuck until he's ready to leave. This is a mistake, I'm sure of it. What should I do?

He looked up at Pangur, who was watching him with fierce green eyes. "Don't even think about it," they seemed to say.

Mati washed his sore leg. It was healing well but his head felt warm, flustered by a light fever that took over his senses and left him dull. In a trance he dipped in and out of the dream-wake, longing for someone to guide him. The spirits were silent.

The fever hummed at Mati's temples. All day he drifted at the Borderlands of Fiâney, tracing the edges of his dreams. He was troubled by memories of the passageway that ran beyond the second gate – the path to Sienta, the land of the first cat. He remembered the power and beauty of Te Bubas, the stillness of the air, the endless calm. He thought of the catling he had seen there, with one eye green, the other amber. He was only vaguely aware of other cats as they passed in and out of the barn, miaowing excitedly to each other. Sparrow appeared with a mouse that Trillion had caught for him, but Mati only blinked at him and returned to the dream-wake.

"Don't you want it?"

Mati looked up. Hovering over him was Domino. Mati followed the catling's gaze to the limp mouse before him. He shook his head. A few paces back stood Sparrow, looking worried.

"What's wrong?" asked Domino.

"I'm tired," said Mati. "But I think..." His eyes trailed across the barn. He spotted Torko and Arabella asleep next to Sinestra, who was washing Ria's ears. Pritin was also resting with her kittens. And there was Pangur, standing at a distance from the others, staring at Mati with cool green eyes.

Mati turned back to Domino and spoke quietly. "I need to leave." Sparrow was too far back to hear him and, sensing that the conversation was private, he walked away to join Daisy. Mati continued. "I am glad that the cats have found a home here. We cannot know the future but... But I feel that they will be safe. That they will be happy." He spoke of "the cats" – he was not including himself in this.

"It's a good place, isn't it? The hinds seem pleased to have mousers. They don't want housecats. Have you noticed that Daisy doesn't wear a collar? It isn't really owning, is it, if she doesn't live with them? I guess she grants socage, in a way, I mean they give her that crunchy meat. But we can fend for ourselves," said Domino proudly. "It's just somewhere to sleep."

Mati agreed.

"Did Pangur tell you that I'm coming with you? We're in this together, fella."

Mati blinked appreciatively. "He did. But your amma's here. Won't you…?"

Domino shook his head. "There comes a time when a cat must stand alone. I will see her again, some day."

Mati wasn't sure that he would, but he didn't say so. "I think we should leave. I think we should go as soon as possible."

"But you need to rest. Your leg—"

"It's nothing," said Mati quickly. He sat up, trying to appear more alert. "It's almost back to normal. I want to go now. Before nightfall." His voice dropped to a whisper. "Pangur won't allow it."

"Can't we wait a day or two?"

Mati's eyes flashed. "No!" he hissed and Domino flinched.

The black-and-white paused a moment, then nodded. "I will talk to my amma." The harlequin catling left to find Trillion, leaving Mati alone once more.

Mati was still crouching in the same spot when Domino returned. Trillion was standing a few paces away, watching sadly, and Pangur was by her side. The other ferals were gathered round, having heard rumours that some of the cats were leaving.

"It's OK," said Domino.

Mati got to his feet. "We're going?"

Domino nodded.

"How did you manage it?"

The black-and-white catling blinked. "I've got ways." He threw a glance at his mother.

Pangur approached the catlings. "Trillion has persuaded me of the urgency. She and her son speak strongly on your behalf. I have taken their comments to heart — we will not delay longer. For the sake of the others, we leave immediately."

There was a sharp intake of breath from several of the watching ferals but Mati sighed with relief.

Pangur turned to them. "It is true. I will be leaving you, together with Mati, Domino and Jess. You will be well looked after by Trillion. Your story shall continue here, in this pleasant place. Ours shall not — for Mati has a journey he must make, and we have agreed to accompany him." Torko opened his mouth, but Pangur silenced him by continuing. "Do not ask where our journey will take us, for none of us can say. But there is a world out there and we intend to be part of it. Perhaps our paths will cross once more..."

Trillion took a step forward and washed Domino's head.

Pangur sighed. "Perhaps they will not. But know that I took great pride in leading the kin, and you cats are the best of it. Friends, there is no time for long farewells, and you should know by now that it's not how I do things." The former chief batted a paw in the air, almost playfully. Like the night that Pangur had led them from Cressida Lock, Mati saw the kitten he used to be: bright and energetic, powerful and good-humoured. "So long, cats," said Pangur. "Good life, good health." True to his word, he turned on his tail and hurried out of the barn where Jess was waiting. Domino broke away from his mother with a little mew and followed him.

Mati cleared his throat. "I am sorry to be leaving... Really sorry. I was alone in the world before Cressida Lock. You welcomed me and protected me. You have shown me the meaning of friendship."

The cats were silent, blinking at him with sad eyes.

Sparrow stepped forward. "You are still so young, Mati. I shouldn't let you do this. Where will you go? What will you eat? Oh, I know I'm fussing but I can't help it." His bad eye squinted shut an instant and he looked away.

"Mr Sparrow, sir. I need to thank you most of all... You have always been so kind to me, right from the beginning. You stood by me; you took my side. How can I ever repay you?" Mati dipped his head. A wave of sadness unsteadied his resolve — dulled the urgency to leave. He remembered that first meeting, in Sparrow's chamber with Domino, Ria and Binjax. Sparrow had offered them kippers, had spoken up for Mati at the full-moon meeting and had gone on to share his home with the catling. He was the closest thing to family that Mati had. How could he think of leaving him?

"Oh, Mati, there is nowt to repay! I have been pleased

of the company, so pleased." Sparrow leaned forward and whispered in the catling's ear. "Truth to be told, I had been a little lonely before you came... I was always glad of your companionship."

Mati lifted his head and rubbed his temple against Sparrow's neck. The thick ginger fur tickled his nose. Sniffing, he noticed Daisy standing with the others, looking at Sparrow with concern. She met Mati's gaze. Again he felt that tug of affection and loss; the same shudder of emotions he had sensed on first meeting the old cat. "Do not worry for your friend," her eyes told him. "I shall take care of him. He won't be alone."

Mati blinked at her in gratitude and stepped away. "You will be happy here, Mr Sparrow," he said. Glancing at the others, he repeated his words. "You will be happy here. I feel it." Then he turned from them and hurried from the barn. He did not look back.

White Moon

Mati, Pangur, Domino and Jess left in silence to circle around the back of the stables, where the long-faced horses stared curiously. The river was out of sight but still nearby as they followed a parallel route across low-cut fields.

Pangur was in the lead. Occasionally, he glanced at Mati, seeking assurance that they were on the right track, but the catling's face was blank. An overcast afternoon lapsed into a dusky evening. Rolling pastures curved downhill, the land beneath growing damper, with the faintest hint of salt on the air. A flock of gulls soared over the sky, their white feathers luminous in the vanishing light. Their sharp cries cut through the silence of the countryside and the cats watched them warily as they passed overhead.

The sun set in the horizon. Half a moon rose in its

cascading light. Eventually, the darkening pastures ended at a high wooden fence. Pangur stopped as the others gathered round. Mati's eyes trailed up the fence and his nose wrinkled. The salty air was more noticeable now and he could smell something else – the faintest whiff of rubber. He pressed the pad of his front paw on the wood as his friends watched him. He felt compelled to cross the fence but another impulse, deeper, fainter, was holding him back.

The others stared at the Tygrine expectantly.

"Over, right?" asked Domino.

Mati was slow to reply. "Over," he said finally, but without conviction.

The cats skittered up the fence easily and sprang down the other side. There the grass grew wild, interrupted only by high trees. The ground was even damper here – almost sodden – a thin layer of mud clung to their paw pads. They wove soundlessly between the tall grasses as crows cawed in branches. Now Mati led the way, racing beneath the trees, despite the dull ache in his back leg. Pangur was just behind him, followed by Jess and Domino. The night took on a mauve tinge. A thin veil of clouds hung over the sky, obscuring the stars. Only the half-moon broke through them, low and perfectly white.

Mati tried to focus on the land that unravelled before them, pushing away the image of the ghostly moon. The eye of the night was only half open, yet it seemed to pulsate with life. It trailed over the fleeing cats.

Eventually they met a waterway as it snaked downstream.

"Is this the same river we were following before?" asked Domino. "Does it come from Cressida Lock?"

Mati shook his head. He didn't think so. It was larger, with rapid water and a saltier smell. Its banks were edged with concrete.

"I didn't know there was more than one," panted the black-and-white.

For a moment Mati remembered the river of his kittenhood, but he pushed the thought away. "There are many."

The river widened. "I think it's an estuary," said Jess.

Pangur turned his eyes on her. "What do you mean?"

She paused beneath his gaze. "It's ... it's where the river meets the sea. My hind told me about it."

"The sea?" gasped Mati. Of course, that explained the salty smell. Forgetting the ache in his leg he hurried faster. What had Etheleldra said? "Run to the sea..." He had instantly forgotten her words, had not planned to reach this place – but somehow he had found it nonetheless. He tracked the river until the land before him was barred by another fence, this one made of wire links and crowned with spiky barbs.

Pangur appeared at his side. "Allow me." He started scrabbling under the wire. The catlings watched as his head disappeared beneath it, his back legs ramming the grassy soil. A moment later he broke through to the other side.

They hastily scurried after him.

The four cats gasped as they scanned the world beyond the boundary. A vast expanse of concrete stretched towards a port. Along it stood towering cranes, forklift trucks and row upon row of parked lorries. Further from the water's edge were coloured metal boxes, each the size of one of the lorries. The scale of this concrete city was difficult to fathom and Mati felt small and insignificant. Wouldn't even a hind feel humbled in this world of giant objects? he wondered. Most of all, he struggled to take in the container ships that rested along the waterfront. He had travelled by ship to a dockyard east of Cressida Lock, but it had been nothing like these monstrous vessels.

Beyond the ships lay open water. A faint light flecked the surface, a silvery reflection of the moon.

Pangur turned to Jess. "Can you see hinds?"

The docks looked deserted. The tortoiseshell-and-white narrowed her eyes. "Those things they move around in... Bigger than the ones on normal roads, but I think it's the same idea. Some have blinking lights. That probably means there are hinds inside."

"What next?" asked Domino, looking to Pangur for guidance. The black tom turned to Mati.

The catling didn't answer immediately. He studied the retreating river beyond the wire fence, then each of his friends' faces. Finally, he took in the giant vessels resting along the port.

The husky voice in his head surprised him. "Yes, Mati. You have guessed it – you know what you must do. The last one, blue with white decks." It was the voice he had heard in Daisy's barn, urging him to leave.

Mati shut his eyes. "Who are you?" he asked silently.

"There is no time now to explain," said the voice. "You must hurry. Trust me…"

Mati's eyes flicked open. His heart began to thud. He had felt a ragged footfall from beyond the wire fence. Somebody – *something* – was coming. This time he spoke out loud, to his friends. "We have to leave. Over the waves."

Pangur frowned. "But how?"

"A ship," said Jess quietly. "You want us to board a ship. Those massive things on the water."

Domino's eyes widened. "But we can't! We can't go on them! What if they sink? They couldn't float for long. Where do they go? Which one? How do we—"

Mati cut him off. "That one." He indicated the last ship in the row, a blue-and-white cargo vessel with at least four distinguishable levels. Coloured containers had been lifted on board by one of the giant cranes, which was now withdrawing. Three humans appeared on the lower deck, talking loudly. Mati started towards them and the other cats followed. He paused a short distance away, out of sight of the humans, listening. "The cargo is loaded," he said. "They're going to remove the gangplank. We need to board now." He took a few steps closer to the ship. Between the vessel

196

and the dockside was a space at least four tail-lengths wide – too far to jump. And with the decks high above, where would they jump to? Ears pressed back, he looked down at the trembling water that separated the ship from the land.

"Where is it going?" asked Pangur.

Mati glanced back. "I didn't hear. Did you, Jess?"

The tortoiseshell-and-white shook her head. Like Mati, she could understand something of human chatter. "I don't think they said. But what's the difference? We wouldn't know what it meant. They use symbols for words, noises without sense. They would not say 'nice place with food, where hinds like cats'. They rarely describe what they mean. They would say a place that we can't possibly imagine. We do not know this world of hinds. How far it reaches; where they go to on their journeys." Her voice trembled. Her words had tumbled out, a lonely mewing in the silence of the night.

"It doesn't matter," said Mati. He knew that his friends were scared – that he was asking a great deal of them – but his senses forbade him to linger. He had only one thought now, and he uttered it urgently: "We have to hurry!" He searched the vessel for a gangplank that would allow them to climb onto the ship, like the one he had used to board the craft from his homeland. Nothing seemed obvious. Then he noticed a row of steep metal steps that extended from one of the high decks down onto the dockside, reaching across shifting waters that divided the ship from the land. They would be difficult to mount – harder than a wooden plank – but what choice did they have?

The humans withdrew from sight.

"We should go now, if we're..." Jess didn't finish.

Mati nodded. He rushed towards the ship with Domino and Jess close behind him. Pangur hung back a moment, watchful. Mati leapt onto the first step of the gangplank, his back legs skidding dangerously. He righted himself and sprang to the next step, heart racing in his chest. Beneath him he could smell the salty water. He turned back. Jess and Domino stood on the dockside, at the bottom of the steps.

"It's totally safe," lied Mati. "Take it one at a time."

Domino nodded and followed him with Jess at his heels. The steps stretched, seemingly endless, each one higher above the perilous seawater, but finally they had reached the top. Mati turned back. Pangur was down on the dockside.

"Why aren't you coming?"

"I am," said Pangur. "It's just – I thought I heard something."

Mati glanced up instinctively and caught the half-moon. It pulsed large and low. A spasm of fear shot through him. His breath caught in his throat and he staggered, as though struck.

Jess was staring at him, alarmed. "Mati, what's wrong?"

He shook his head, struggling to breathe. As he looked back at Pangur he saw the air beyond grow hazy. It was almost as if it was scorched – as though it had burned thin. The city of tarmac, cranes and lorries grew vague before his eyes. And there appeared the shadow creature, emerging from the darkness. It moved in leaps and twists, coiling into itself upon landing; pouncing forward in a fractured, crazed advance. Several sets of teeth flickered in the moonlight; six ghoulish eyes; three slashing tails. Yet it was one being – one shuddering, leaping mass.

Pangur had seen it too. He froze on the dockside, paws splayed.

Mati couldn't speak. A strangled sound escaped his throat. This was no cat – not a feline of this world, the land of the first self. It was something from the dream-wake, a wraith, a phantom. But how could it be – how could a creature of Fiåney exist in the physical realm?

Jess was at Mati's side. "Hurry, Pangur, hurry!" she cried over the drone of the engines.

Domino stared beyond Pangur at the twisting, loping creature. "What *is* it?"

The ground beneath their paws began to quake.

"The steps!" gasped Jess. "They're moving." She and Domino leapt back in unison, onto the solid deck. Some motorized force was at work on the gangplank and it started to fold against the side of the ship. Mati was glued to the top step.

"Mati?" Domino called to him. "Help me," he told Jess. Together they craned forward, gripping their friend by the scruff and yanking him roughly onto the deck.

Domino pawed at Mati but the Tygrine didn't move, golden eyes frozen in horror.

Jess had turned back to the docks. *"Pangur!"*

The black tom swung his face towards the metal steps, to the ship and the catlings that stared down at him. "This is my fault," he said. "I wouldn't let you leave. Mati warned me—"

"What's that you say?" called Domino. They couldn't hear him beyond the whirr of the engines.

Mati sat, dumb, unblinking. His eyes were fixed on the phantom. He could not guess what it was, or how it had entered the world of the first self. But he had known from the first time he had sensed its approach at Cressida Lock, and felt the frantic beating of its paws through the ground. *He had known that it would find him.*

Down on the dockside the creature hissed and spat, gathering momentum beneath the throbbing moon. It caught sight of Mati and, realizing that the metal steps were collapsing against the side of the ship, sped frantically towards them, ignoring Pangur. It moved with impossible speed, jerking and leaping onto the bottom step as it rose into the air.

"It's here!" miaowed Domino. *"It's here!"*

Terror tightened around Mati's throat. The creature was tail-lengths away. It had found him. It would set upon Mati, would shatter the third pillar – would enslave the spirit of every living cat. They had left it too late. The ship was leaving but the creature had made it: *it was almost on board!*

Mati's thoughts were spinning but his body had turned to stone. He watched as Pangur's eyes flashed green and brilliant, as the powerful tom sprang off the dockside and launched himself onto the bottom step. His front paws landed on the phantom, hugging it with his claws. It bucked furiously from his grip and he struggled against it, flinging himself higher up its jerking spine as the metal steps rose over the water, tilting at an angle against the ship.

Pangur's eyes closed and his mouth screwed into an agonized grimace, as though the phantom's touch scalded his flesh. The creature hissed furiously, spitting with rage, thrashing innumerable paws. Pangur's grip tightened. Beneath the pitchy shimmer of his fur, his muscles tensed. For a moment his grimace faded and he was triumphant: a chief among ferals; a leader defiant and brave. The tomcat cried out – his voice reaching over the droning engines. Then he and the phantom fell backwards off the edge of the folding metal step – down to the silvery waters below.

The great ship stirred in a storm of spray and pulled away into the night.

The
Third
Gate

The Suzerain's Discovery

The Suzerain's scream exploded in his chamber and rang through the palace of the Sa Mau. High priests fled along the shaded corridors while sentinels cowered in dread. Out in the city of Zagazig, alley cats scurried beneath parked cars.

Humans were indifferent to the distant yowl of an angry cat – other animals were more sensitive. A donkey brayed while its owner tugged at its rope. A pack of stray dogs whined and backed away, tails curling between their legs. A caged mynah bird squawked in terror as sparrows flapped over the city streets.

The world of the second self was also rocked by the Suzerain's fury. The scream shuddered through Fiâney, stirring the spirits from their silence.

"My Lord, what haunts thee?" It was Great Spirit Alia, the

Suzerain's staunchest ally in the other realm.

"O Alia, Alia, I have been wronged! The mission has failed! The slayers I sent have drowned in the ocean and the Tygrine has escaped!"

"Whisht, My Lord, have faith in Fiåney. Too readily you despair."

"Yet it is so, Noble Spirit – I know it to be so! I cannot be deceived. They fell into water. They plunged from a height and descended to the deeps."

"Yes," agreed the spirit.

"They are defeated! Their mission has failed!"

Great Spirit Alia was patient. She spoke softly. "You forget what they are. For they are not forged of the elements. They are not of the first self."

"They are spirits, like you," said the Suzerain. "Not of your worth," he added hastily, "but of your world. How Ipanel begged me not to release them; how Lamet rebuked this desperate act. I cast her out, banished her from the kingdom. Perhaps I acted hastily. It seems I was mistaken."

"You made no mistake, My Lord. It is true that the Three are spirits of Fiåney – creatures of the second self. And how, O Sire, might one kill a spirit?" The halls of the dream-wake murmured amid a dim encircling mist.

The Suzerain frowned, his brow lowered in thought. Outside his chamber, in the land of the first self, the sentinels heard nothing of this discussion. They did not enter Fiåney, did not conspire in these secret affairs. They knew

206

only that the scream had stilled and they held their breaths. Perhaps the Master's wrath was spent at last.

The Cat Lord sat for a while in silent contemplation. Great Spirit Alia did not disturb his thoughts but he knew she was there, waiting for him. Finally he raised his head. When he spoke again, his voice was quiet and controlled once more. "Spirits are not *alive* – they have no bodies of flesh. They are not creatures of the first self."

"You speak wisdom, My Lord."

"Spirits are the essence of cat. They exist only in Fiåney – or they did until I released the Three."

"You changed the natural order of things, My Lord. By the power of the moon."

"The Three do not live and..." his voice fell to a whisper, straining with suppressed excitement. "And so they *cannot die*." The true significance of this dawned on the Suzerain. "They are driven by only one will, the one that I instilled in them, and that is to destroy the Tygrine. He cannot kill them – no one can. Not even I."

"Nor I," agreed Great Spirit Alia.

"But unlike the Three, the Tygrine is made of flesh and fur. He exists in the physical realm."

"You are a sage, My Lord."

"My spirits shall never surrender and they cannot be killed. They will follow the Tygrine to the ends of the earth. They will find him by the eye of the moon."

"They will do what Mithos should have, Wise Master.

They will destroy the Tygrine cat."

The Suzerain's voice rose in elation. "Yes! Then conquest will be mine, for I shall own the feline soul! Your loyalty will be rewarded a thousand fold. The reign of the Tygrine will be over for ever and together we shall rule over Fiåney and earth."

"One Law," murmured the spirit.

"One Law," repeated the Suzerain.

The Mournful Sea

The halls of Fiåney were grey, like dawn over a frozen valley. Walking through them alone, Mati shivered.

"To have is to lose, the earth was soon to learn. And so I too learned."

The words of Te Bubas touched Mati's second self. He felt her presence circling him, invisible to the eye but tangible to the senses. She tried to reach out to him, to comfort the broken catling. Deep within the velvet of her voice he felt safe.

"Two kits were born from my lonely tears. Two kits who brought me such joy. From them sprang the hope of future generations, the promise of immortality. I bathed them in my love; I offered them my heart. I did not know of tragedy then – could not have guessed what was to come.

"But all was not lost, Mati," the first cat said. "I thought the world had ended but it did not end for me. It continued, unmoved by my suffering. Just as now it cannot pity you nor share the sorrow that you feel."

"Pangur knew that he would die. He must have known," said Mati.

"He acted with great courage."

"Aren't I the Tygrine cat, protector of the third pillar? I should have saved him. I failed. I let him—"

"A greater purpose beckons you, young cat. It is not your time."

"It wasn't his time either," Mati whimpered.

"Perhaps it was. He urged you, compelled you to stay when your instincts ordered you to flee. He is not guilty of the cruelty that slew him, but he understood the role that he played in that bitter confrontation. He longed to atone for these mistakes, to win back the honour he was born to. And so he has. He died a noble cat."

"How do you know all that?"

"That, and more besides. I know that the young and the powerful fall. Treachery exists in the land of the first self. In Fiåney too. Not even the innocent are spared."

"It isn't fair!" the catling wailed. "It isn't *fair*."

"No, my child. It is not fair. I have seen enough to despair many times, and yet I keep faith. Live justice through your thoughts and deeds but do not seek it in this life."

"We were all so happy at Cressida Lock… Why did that have to change?"

"I do not know. Perhaps the constant flux of the earth is what keeps it in motion. Change is one of our only certainties. And so we move between pain and sorrow, elation and joy."

"If we could find that moment of joy. If we could hold onto it..."

Te Bubas sounded wistful. "That moment of joy," she murmured. "Well, then, the sedicia flowers would always bloom — not just for an instant lost to time. All wrongs would be forgiven, all pain erased. But that cannot be."

Mati's heart ached with grief. "*Why* did Pangur have to leave us? Can't you give it some meaning?"

"Your friend died with dignity and honour. He did not doubt the rightness of his actions. Take comfort, child. The paths of the dream-wake are limitless. There are pastures in Fiåney where the grass grows thick and the sun shines in eternal summer. None can age and no one dies. It is the land of memory, and within it our fallen friends shall live for ever."

"Take me there, please take me," Mati begged.

"The land is within you. If you wish to, you can go there. You can go there any time."

"Really? But how?"

"It is Ra'ha, the realm beyond the third gate, and it lies deep within your second self. Even as you forget, it waits and hopes to welcome you. You will go there when you are ready. Now you must return to your first self, to your body. You are needed."

"No!" cried Mati. "I want to go to Ra'ha now! I don't want to go back."

He felt the air grow thin around him and knew that she had gone. The heat from his paws waned. His second self stood alone in mists of Fiåney. His first self was curled in a tight ball beneath a series of pipes on the ship's enormous deck. The vessel hardly stirred on the water but he felt each tremor like an earthquake. His ears pressed back, drowning out the world around him: the wind that crept beneath the pipes to ruffle his fur; the chill of the metal deck. He wanted to hide in the dream-wake, to find that land where the sun always shone, where summer never ended. Where no one died.

Voices were speaking over him.

"He's had a shock."

"We all have. Pangur... I still don't believe he's gone."

"He stopped that *thing*. He died a hero, and the kin don't even know."

"It's better that way. It would pain them. Let them remember him as he was in life."

Mati opened his eyes. Domino and Jess were crouched next to him beneath the pipes.

"Thank goodness you're awake, you worried us!" Jess berated.

Mati licked his muzzle. "Sorry," he said in a small voice. Sorry I did nothing, he thought, sorry I fell apart. Sorry I didn't... "Pangur?"

212

"He is gone," said Domino, eyes downcast.

"I hoped... I hoped that I'd imagined it."

Jess shook her head. "It's so hard to believe. He seemed indestructible."

"He took that thing with him," said Domino. "That *monster*."

Mati nodded. They were safe – safe from the phantom, in any event – but the cost had been terrible. It was impossible to think that Pangur had drowned, that he wouldn't appear in a moment, sauntering towards them, glossy tail held high. Mati winced at the memory, and at the words of Te Bubas in his mind: "To have is to lose."

Domino interrupted his thoughts. "What were they – *it?* Did you know that ... that it was coming? Is that what we were running from? Are they... Is it anything to do with that other tribe?"

"The Sa Mau? I think so." Mati didn't want to say any more. Why scare his friends now the danger had passed? What would it help if he told them that the phantom was a creature of Fiåney, committed to destroying him and the third pillar, the spirit of all cats?

Domino's eyes brightened. "That means we can go home! We can find the others on Daisy's farm. Amma will be so happy! There'll be that nice dry food that the hinds leave out, and Amma will catch a mouse for me."

Mati stared ahead. He rose on trembling paws and eased his way out from beneath the pipes. The others followed him. Above them climbed stairways to other parts of the ship, and further decks disappeared below. Somewhere on the awesome vessel would be humans, creatures that could not be trusted, hidden beyond metal walls.

The catlings stepped carefully towards the railing, shivering against the wind. White-tipped water thrashed against the ship, streaking it with bubbling foam. The first gleam of dawn rose from the east, lighting the sea that rolled into the distance.

Mati glanced at the others. Jess met his gaze with her knowing green eyes. It was she who spoke the words that would break Domino's heart.

"We're not going back. Not ever."

Perched on a deck of the massive ship, the three young cats were tiny figures, lost against the limitless sprawl of the sea.

What the Moon Knows

The catlings caught a few hours of uncomfortable sleep, curled up against each other beneath the pipes. When Mati opened his eyes he saw that night had passed at last. Clouds still hung in an overcast sky but even this dull light stung his eyes as he crept from under the pipes and stepped onto the whitewashed deck.

He lapped at a puddle of rainwater along the metal grooves beneath his paws. He had been aboard a ship before, the one that saved him from the Army of the Sa Mau, which had taken him away from his homeland. It had been smaller and he had stowed away near the kitchen, where scraps were always available for a quick meal. This ship was different. Mati guessed that there would be food for the humans somewhere but he couldn't work out a way of accessing it. How long would it take the ship to reach land – if it ever did? What would they eat in the meantime?

He heard the sound of boots plodding over metal and scrambled back under the pipes.

"I'll do this deck," called a human voice. A moment later a man in overalls appeared, carrying a mop and bucket. He started cleaning enthusiastically.

"OK, I'll head to the upper deck," another voice replied from further away. Mati could just see the shape of a second man as he crossed towards the metal stairs and climbed them until he was out of sight.

Jess and Domino had awoken and watched, with Mati, their tails drooped low. The remaining man maintained his energetic mopping for a few more moments. Then, pausing to look up towards the higher deck, he fumbled inside his overalls and pulled out a packet of cigarettes.

"What's he doing?" asked Domino.

The sailor leaned on the mop, smoking and staring out to sea.

"I don't know," said Jess. "It's a strange life for a hind. I can't imagine they really like it this far away from land. Some of them have kins. Perhaps they have left their young behind."

"Then why do they do it?" said Domino.

Jess shrugged. The sailor turned, flicked his cigarette over the side of the deck and resumed his mopping with less vigour than before. He started making his way towards the pipes under which the catlings crouched. He paused, scratching his head.

"He's seen us!" hissed Mati. They scrambled further beneath the pipes.

The man crouched down, frowning. After a few moments he stood and started washing the deck once more, working away from them.

Eventually, the other sailor reappeared, heading down the metal steps from the upper deck. "Everything OK?"

"Yes, fine." The first man paused. "Mick, listen to this. I thought I saw something. It moved over there."

"Something *moved?*"

"There aren't any rats here, are there?"

"No way! There are rat guards on all the ropes. No chance a rat's getting on. Don't tell Captain, he'll make us deep clean top to bottom and there's no point."

"Guess not." The first man didn't sound sure.

"You're losing it!" laughed the second man. "Come on, breakfast."

The two sailors disappeared around the deck. The catlings heard a creaking sound as a hatch opened, followed by a clang as it shut behind them.

Mid-morning the hatch creaked again. The sailor who had been mopping their deck reappeared and approached the pipes. The catlings had remained hidden so he couldn't see them.

217

The man knelt down. "There was definitely something," he mumbled. "Mick can laugh all he likes." Out of his overalls he pulled a small bundle, wrapped in a serviette. Reaching under the pipes he dropped the contents on the deck. It was a congealed lump of omelette. He shuffled backwards and watched.

"Smell that!" whispered Domino. "Yum!"

"Shhh!" Jess scolded. "He'll hear you miaowing!"

"What if he does? He seems friendly."

"It could be a trap!"

Domino sniffed and took a couple of steps towards the piece of omelette.

"Get back here!" hissed Jess but the harlequin catling ignored her.

"Be careful," urged Mati, more weakly.

Domino stepped cautiously towards the food, sniffed it a moment and took a bite.

The man stared in amazement. "It's a little cat!"

Domino looked up at him.

"Oh no," muttered Jess. "That idiot."

"Here, kitty," called the sailor, reaching out his hand. Domino approached to sniff his fingertips. He licked them gingerly.

"You're just like Midnight, my cat at home!" said the man.

Domino could not have understood these words, but he recognized the friendly tone and started rubbing his face against the man's hand. The sailor responded by stroking

218

his head. Then he pulled back his hand and watched as Domino took a few eager bites of omelette.

"You can't stay here," said the sailor. "We're not allowed pets. All that rabies stuff. There'll be a stack of red tape if Captain finds out. British authorities would stick you in quarantine. I wouldn't do that to you."

Behind him was the sound of the metal hatch creaking. The sailor stood up quickly and Domino withdrew beneath the pipes, alarmed.

"Don't let anyone see you," whispered the sailor. "I'll come back, Midnight. I'll get you more to eat. Just keep hidden." He took a few steps away from the pipes and spoke in a different voice. "Chief Officer Henric, am I needed inside?"

Another man appeared at the far side of the deck. "Captain wants you to check the container lists."

The two men disappeared back through the hatch and the catlings were alone again.

Jess turned angrily on Domino. "What were you thinking? Now they'll all know that we're here. They'll catch us! They'll—"

"He was nice!" cried Domino. "He liked me. He had food."

Mati watched them. He had said little since Pangur's death.

Jess's ears flicked back. "Didn't I tell you that you only think with your stomach? He was trying to trap you!"

Domino looked doubtful. "What did he say?"

"He said you reminded him of his cat," said Mati. The others turned to look at him.

"What does that mean?" asked Domino.

"It's a trick," said Jess. "We could move to a different part of the ship. It's big enough. We shouldn't stay here – he'll be back."

Domino was triumphant. "Back to bring me more grub!"

"Back with others to catch us and throw us overboard!"

Domino's jaw slackened. "He was friendly..."

"My hind's daughter was friendly when she tried to lure me into the carrying cage. Her intentions weren't. Oh no, far from it."

"So that's what you reckon – that this hind will come back with others?"

"That's what I said, isn't it?"

"Well let's wait and see. If he comes with others, we hide. If he comes alone, we can trust him."

"You can't trust any of them."

"You trusted your hind," Domino pointed out, "the one you owned."

"That's different."

"Different how?"

"I knew him. He was kind."

"Well I'll get to know this one."

"It's *different*," Jess insisted.

The catlings lapsed into silence. Overhead the clouds sank closer to the sea. The sky darkened and rain started falling on the whitewashed deck. It landed with light taps, gathering in puddles. Mati shivered, backing further beneath the pipes. He remembered Te Bubas's words: "There are pastures in Fiåney where the grass grows thick and the sun shines in eternal summer."

"There's still a bit of food left," said Domino. He indicated the omelette. "It's getting wet. I've had some, you should finish it."

Mati turned away and sank onto his belly, folding his front paws beneath him.

Jess met Domino's eye but she said nothing.

Mati curled up into a tight ball and gazed at the murky green sea. Domino had gone to explore the deck and Jess was washing herself nearby. It had stopped raining but the sky was overcast and grey.

Jess ran a tortoiseshell-and-white paw over her face. "Mati … there's something that I've been meaning to tell you. I suppose I didn't mention it before because you had enough to worry about, but I see you doubting yourself … and you shouldn't. You were right to leave Cressida Lock. When I arrived there, trying to find you, the place had changed."

"Changed?" Mati's ears twitched.

"Oh, it looked just the same. But it didn't *feel* the same. It was all wrong. Like a cloud had passed over it."

"What about Binjax? What did he say?"

Jess paused. "Binjax? I didn't see him. That's the point, Mati. *I didn't see anyone.*"

"But they stayed on the market-place. Binjax, Fink, the others... Only a small group of us left with Pangur."

"Well they weren't there when I arrived. The hinds were all business as usual, like nothing had happened. But I didn't see any of the kin."

"No cats?" asked Mati, taking this in.

"Not even a whisker." Jess glanced across the deck. "I don't have your senses. I don't know much. But it felt bad there, and it scared me."

"The phantom," said Mati. He didn't look up. "The phantom got to the market-place." Silently, he hoped that the cats had escaped, that they were safe. He thought of Binjax. The silver tabby was stubborn. He would have remained at Cressida Lock. He wouldn't have understood the danger.

Poor Binjax, thought Mati. Poor, proud tabby. Mati's mind drifted to Sinestra. She had known, with a mother's instinct: she had guessed her son's sad end.

"Don't you see?" said Jess. "You were right all along. We shouldn't have delayed at Daisy's barn. You wanted to go straight away, didn't you? You can't blame yourself for that. Your judgement never let you down, and you never failed the kin. It isn't your fault, you know."

"What?" murmured Mati.

"Pangur ... it isn't your fault."

Mati blinked. He wanted to share his feelings with Jess

but the words stayed inside him, spinning through his mind. I didn't protect him, he thought. I was scared. I froze. I did nothing – I didn't even try. I was a coward and because of me a great cat fell. Now there's no one to protect us.

He remembered the honourable cats that he'd known, in his own world and the dream-wake. His mother, who had faced the Sa Mau, her power sapped, giving up her life to protect her son and the friends she left behind. Te Bubas, the first cat who walked the earth, who existed in the land of Sienta, through the dream-wake's second gate. His real father had died on Mati's first day on earth – that is what the spirit Bayo had told him. And now the cat that Mati longed to think of as a father – the former chief of the Cressida Cats – had died too. The phantom had drowned with him, but the Suzerain was out there, somewhere, hungering to destroy the Tygrine line.

Mati stared out to sea but his eyes were blank. The world felt immense – too big for a small cat. He missed the comfort of Sparrow's chamber and his easy warmth. What was the ginger tom doing now? Mati wondered. He thought of Daisy. She would look after his old friend.

Jess lowered her paw. "Did you hear me?"

Mati raised his face. Under the shadow of the pipes and the dim light of an overcast sky, his eyes looked as cloudy as the water. "Where does the moon go during the day?" he asked.

Jess had grown up among humans, living alone with an

old man for much of her life. Her ideas about the world were unlike those of the ferals. Still, she knew what most cats believed: that the armies of the day fought the armies of the night. That the moon led the battles as twilight fell and was vanquished every morning as the sun reappeared. "I couldn't tell you," she answered honestly.

"It scares me."

"The moon?"

"It knows."

Jess's ears flicked back. "What does it know?"

Mati lowered his face and shut his eyes.

Jess watched her friend. "What does it know?" she repeated.

The Tygrine's body was perfectly still. He had retreated into a trance, had travelled into Fiåney. Into space, silence and searching shadows. Into a place where she could not follow.

Reborn

Afternoon faded into evening, and evening turned to night. A mantle of cloud hung over the sky and few stars glanced through the darkness. The moon was hidden, floating beyond the eye's reach.

The cargo ship cruised effortlessly over the black water. It passed no other carriers, cutting its lonely course through the ocean. The ceaseless waves hurried alongside it in curls of froth.

The dockyard was already leagues away, a distant city of towering cranes and blinking lights. Along the furthest edge of the dockside, near the high fence and the nature reserve, a fluorescent bulb flickered. Clinging to the shadows, a creature hauled itself along the concrete, shaking out its matted fur. It rose from the ground, hissing, furious, flexing misshapen limbs. From a distance, it might have looked like a number of cats. Several sets of teeth flashed in the gloom; six ghoulish eyes; three slashing tails. Yet it was one being – one shuddering, quivering mass.

The phantom was back.

A Harlequin's Friend

The sailor did not return until the next morning. He walked towards the pipes and knelt down, eyes narrowed.

He squinted into the shadows. "Midnight? Midnight?" he called in a low voice.

"Can I go to him?" Domino asked.

Mati shrugged.

Jess shook her head. "Don't!"

The harlequin catling frowned. "I think it's OK. I'm going over."

"Fool," she hissed.

Domino ignored her and stalked cautiously towards the sailor.

"Midnight!" he exclaimed. "Here, boy, I brought some chicken from last night. You like chicken, don't you?"

Domino began to purr, rubbing his face against the man's outstretched hand.

"I'll bring you more. Don't you worry, Midnight. I'll take care of you." The sailor set down the chicken and watched as Domino caught it between his teeth and dragged it under the pipes. Mati and Jess held back, watching eagerly from the shadows. "Don't let Captain or the others catch you," laughed the sailor. "They wouldn't see the funny side. It's OK, I've got myself on the cleaning rota through the Suez. I'll worry about what to do with you after that. Try not to make a mess, yeah?"

Domino glanced up at him, not understanding the words but appreciating the hospitable tone.

The sailor stood up with a sigh and disappeared through the hatch.

Domino turned to the others. "Tuck in!"

The catlings inched closer. This was no leftover piece of omelette – it was a decent portion of roast chicken – and the smell was irresistible.

"The hind said a destination," said Mati suddenly, mid-bite.

Jess nodded. "But didn't I say that they talk in symbols? How does it help when we haven't the first idea where the place is and what it's like?"

Mati nodded, she had a point. How would they know when to disembark? His mother's words sprang into his mind:

228

"A cat's instincts are the mainstay of his survival. This is the first pillar."

Wasn't it instinct that had led him away from Cressida Lock, that had brought him to the dockyard, to this particular ship? Then he remembered: a voice had urged him to board the ship. A male spirit, but not Bayo – who had it been? Mati frowned. Perhaps he would never find out – he would just have to trust to instinct when the time came.

Every day after that, the sailor appeared with morsels for Domino. He could not have known that other cats also fed on what he left, as only the black-and-white came forward. Domino left any bones beneath the first pipe nearest to the open deck, while the other catlings hid. The man was always careful to clean up afterwards, appearing with his mop and bucket, keen that the other seafarers would not discover his secret. He was generous in his portions, but there was never quite enough to eat. By the fourth sunset, the catlings were thinner.

One afternoon as they finished sharing a piece of white fish, Domino mused. "Did you see how Amma caught all those mice?" He stared dreamily towards the rolling sea.

Jess glanced at him. "You'll taste mouse again, I'm sure." She added no words of comfort about Trillion.

They slept through the days on the ship to the constant moan of the sea. At night they explored the deck but avoided the stairways to other levels. Mati's back leg scarcely troubled him any more. Time merged endlessly, devoid of focus as the vessel steamed ahead. The days grew warmer, the light brighter. Occasionally they passed another ship and the crew appeared on deck, waving, grateful for evidence of life beyond the metal railings.

Mati found a deep stillness in Fiåney. There he walked a desert of glittering sand, searching for the young cat he had once seen in Sienta. Recalling her angular face and the spotted curve of her back. Picturing those unusual eyes, one golden, one green. Remembering how she had left him there, left him to run with the first cat.

A glimpse of land came unexpectedly, at dawn. Already members of the crew were pouring out of the hatch, barking instructions over the wind. The sun baked the white deck, brilliant in a clear blue sky. Gulls circled overhead, their ugly shrieks shattering days of silence.

The catlings were wide awake, crouching beneath the pipes. Mati glanced at the others and took a step forward, his front paw raised and hovering indecisively.

"Are we leaving?" asked Domino.

Mati didn't answer straight away. His ears flat, his haunches low, he submitted his thoughts to Fiåney. And then he heard the husky voice of that unfamiliar spirit. "Not now," he heard. "Not yet."

Over the next two days, the sailor still appeared with food, but his visits became more sporadic and he seemed distracted. A new energy was aboard the ship during the day, a sense of activity. Only the catlings scarcely moved, concealed beneath the pipes.

The ship docked several times. Each landing was the same – Mati would lapse into his own thoughts before concluding that they should stay. And so it came as a surprise to the other catlings when finally, one bright morning, he announced that it was time to leave.

While the humans busied themselves nearby, fastening containers on a higher deck, the catlings dashed out from under the pipes. Land pitched towards them as the sun peeked over a row of warehouses.

"Are we really going?" asked Domino.

Mati glanced at him. He sensed his friend's reluctance, the harlequin catling's new-found bond with the human who brought them food.

"Yes." Mati hadn't expected to feel so certain. The land pulled at him, beckoned him desperately, and he couldn't wait to greet it.

They reached the steel steps at the edge of the deck to find them raised, folded against the side of the ship. Backing away, they hid behind a container. That's right, thought Mati, they had only raised the metal steps just before the ship left land. They'll probably only lower it once we've really arrived.

He waited, flanked by his friends, hidden a short distance

from the collapsible metal steps. It took a surprisingly long time for the vessel to be secured to the dock and when it was, there were humans everywhere. The catlings hunkered against the container, frozen, as people hurried across the deck and down onto the dockside.

It was almost noon before Mati spoke. "Now." He stepped out furtively, neck craned, and slunk towards the top of the metal steps. There were plenty of humans on the dockside but they were gathered among the shadows, and suddenly Mati realized how hot it was. He had hardly noticed the temperature creep up but now it hit him. The sun was searing. It heated the pads of his paws as he stood on deck and, turning to look at his friends, he registered the discomfort in their faces. The uncoated metal stairway would be worse. He paused a moment before launching down it, scrambling awkwardly. The metal was scorching. Beneath the steps shifted the sea, blue, opaque, inestimably deep.

Don't think about it, thought Mati, focus on getting off this thing. Each treacherous step brought back memories of Pangur's final struggle, of the tom's courage, triumph and terror, and Mati's heart ached. If only, he thought... If only Pangur was still at Cressida Lock; if only he had stayed in Daisy's barn; if only I had saved him.

Soon after, the three cats were down on the dockside, resting in the shade of a building. There they washed their sore paws.

"Thank goodness we're off that thing," said Jess, gazing at

232

the immense ship. She looked around her and gasped. "But how different it is here."

Mati blinked his agreement. Everything was blanched in sunlight. The huge cranes that loomed over the docks wore a skin of orange rust and the concrete ground was cracking in a number of places. An unfamiliar smell of spice floated on the air.

Tethered with colourful ropes to a crumbling building stood three of the strangest animals that Mati had ever seen. Each had a single hump on its back and shaggy, sand-coloured fur. They towered on knobbly-kneed legs as their dark eyes rolled over the dockyard. Even from where the cats were sitting, their pungent smell was unmissable.

Mati's nose crinkled. "Horses?"

"I don't think so," said Jess, but she didn't offer an alternative.

Some of the humans milling about the dock were dressed like those they had seen in the past, but others looked different. Gathered in pools of shadow, Mati noticed a group of men in floor-length blue or cream gowns, their heads covered with white turbans. He wondered about this. Wouldn't all that material make them hotter, like an extra layer of fur?

"Where to?" asked Domino. "I'm really hungry, are you? Maybe we could..." His words trailed off. He'd spotted the sailor who had brought him food and started towards him. "Might get a last bite out of the hind."

The man was striding alone along the dockside carrying a

large holdall bag over his shoulder. He was still wearing the same sort of clothes as the others had on the ship – fabric trousers and a separate top – and this set him apart from the men in robes. He noticed Domino with surprise. "Midnight? Is that you?"

Domino miaowed, drawing closer.

"What's he doing?" hissed Jess, turning to Mati.

Mati rose to his paws. "Let's go," he called. He and Jess began along the dockside.

Domino miaowed back. "Hang on!"

Jess paused ahead of Mati as they watched Domino approach the sailor, harlequin tail raised high. The man crouched down and ruffled Domino's head, saying something in quiet tones that the black-and-white could not understand and his friends could not hear.

The men in gowns were huddled in the shadows and did not look over. Mati stared at them, struck by a sudden insight. Perhaps they covered themselves to protect their skin against the sun. After all, he thought, they don't have fur, and the sun is burning hot here. Suddenly, these men made sense – at any rate, he felt he understood them a little bit better.

"I knew it!" Jess was on her haunches, fur on end. Mati shot round. The sailor had scooped up Domino and was carrying him off. The black-and-white started to struggle, realizing what was happening, but the man just tightened his grip.

"Now, now, Midnight, relax!" said the sailor. "It's time to go home."

Domino growled, jerking helplessly, trying to free himself. Spotting his friends, he cried out. "Mati, Jess! Come quick, he's taking me!"

Obelghast

The sailor was moving swiftly over the splitting concrete, kicking up billows of dust. He made his way to a white car that was parked at the edge of the dockyard, at the start of a road. Domino struggled more furiously as Mati and Jess started after them.

Another man leaned out of the open front window of the car. He shook his head when he saw Domino. "La, la!" he called out.

"It's a good cat, very clean," said the sailor.

"Take cat, more cost."

"How much?"

"A hundred and fifty pounds."

"To town? Are you crazy?" The sailor tightened his hold around the black-and-white cat.

"Cat make mess."

"He's good, clean! I'll pay forty pounds Egyptian, no more."

The driver shook his head. "For forty pounds you take camel. You want taxi, a hundred pounds. I do special price. Nice cat."

Jess's ears flicked back. "If they set off on the road we'll never catch them!"

Mati quailed, remembering only vaguely how he had stepped onto the road that ran around Cressida Lock. A car had struck him, had almost killed him. And now his friend was headed for one.

The sailor continued to argue over the fare with the taxi driver, unaware of Mati and Jess's approach. "You are joking me!" he said impatiently. "I will give you sixty pounds – it's a very good price."

"For you, my friend, I take eighty pounds. Nice cat, good cat."

Domino growled, as though making his contribution to the negotiations.

The sailor clicked his tongue. "Seventy pounds. Final offer."

The driver nodded, leaned back in his seat and unlocked the back door, shoving it open. The sailor shrugged off the holdall and stepped one foot inside, still holding Domino firmly.

Mati yowled with a burst of energy, racing up the concrete as the men in gowns turned their heads to gaze from the shadows. He sprang onto the sailor's leg and grasped it with his unsheathed claws, sinking his teeth into his calf. Jess was right behind him. She scrambled up the man's thigh, clinging to the fabric of his trousers.

The sailor yelped, stumbling against the car. His grip on Domino loosened and the harlequin catling scrambled free, miaowing loudly. The three young cats were off like a shot, tearing across the concrete dockyard.

"Midnight?" called the man from the ship. "Midnight, come back!"

From the shadows, the men in gowns watched as the cats sprinted by. One leaned over to another, pointing at the russet-furred catling.

"Cats!" said the driver cheerfully. "They be free animals. Do what they like."

The sailor sighed. He turned to the driver. "Twenty pounds to town. Take it or leave it."

The driver frowned but seeing that he had lost his bargaining chip, he grudgingly agreed.

The catlings passed alongside rows of crates, between the gap in a wire fence and across some scrubland. Beneath the bowing branches of a sycamore fig tree, on the outskirts of a city, they came to a stop.

"I'm sorry," panted Domino, head lowered. "I thought we'd get another feed out of him. I guess it's true, you can't trust them."

He threw a cautious glance at Jess but her eyes were blank.

"It's OK. Hinds are..." Mati chose his words thoughtfully. "Well, it's hard to make sense of them." He looked up. The sun was blazing but was that the very faintest trace of the moon he saw, floating in the sky?

With Domino and Jess by his side, Mati closed his eyes. He had led them into a world of awesome heat, far away from the land they knew. Already Domino had almost been kidnapped, and what other hazards were lurking around the corner? Yet now Mati felt stuck, unsure where to go next. He had no sense of what he was looking for, only a hope – an intuition – that Fiåney would guide him.

The moment he shut his eyes it called to him, inviting him to step inside. He stood in its darkness, hidden from the sun's gaze, far from his friends despite their closeness to him. He pictured, quite faintly, a sandy hilltop with a small mound of rocks and the valley where he'd seen the first cat.

A voice came to him: "I will lead you." It was low and gravelly. Mati had heard it before in Daisy's barn, urging him to leave, and on the docks, telling him to board the ship.

"Thank you but ... who are you?" Mati didn't want to sound rude but he still remembered Etheleldra's warning: not everyone in Fiåney could be trusted.

"My name is Obelghast," intoned the spirit. "I have been

watching you during your journeys to the dream-wake. You need have no fear of my counsel."

"Thank you, Mr Spirit. I am sure you are good."

"It is wise to be wary. Do not take my honesty for granted. Remember the pillars."

"Judgement, the second pillar."

"Exactly, young cat. And what can you glean about me with the pillars in mind? What do your instinct and judgement tell you?"

Mati didn't answer immediately. He reached through Fiåney. His instincts brushed against Obelghast with a whisker's touch. He detected wisdom and kindness, friendship and humour. He thought that he could sense something of the spirit's former appearance, long ago when he was a mortal cat – a large tom with thoughtful amber eyes.

"I trust you," said Mati.

"I am pleased of it, for I wish to assist you, if you will let me. I do not offer you tribal loyalty. I am not faithful to the Tygrine or the Sa. Yet I promised a friend – a cat from the waking world – that I would be her senses in Fiåney. Now I cannot find her in this realm. Instead I meet you and feel the need to protect you. I can not know what my friend would wish… Perhaps I do her wrong by helping you. But treachery stirs, even in these hallowed halls, and I cannot observe it in silence."

Mati was unsettled by Obelghast's words. The spirit sounded confused, and it surprised the catling. Did spirits doubt their actions? Weren't they always simply *sure?* Mati cleared his throat. "Your friend, is she a shalian? I know a queen called Etheleldra—"

The spirit silenced him. "It is not safe to befriend shalians any more – take heed."

"Why?" asked Mati.

"It is not even prudent to talk of them. Know only that my friend is younger than a shalian but was born wise. She is called Lamet."

"Lamet?" Mati had heard that name before, but where? Was it in Fiåney?

"Perhaps you have not heard of her. It is better that way. Enough that you should trust me, by your own instincts, with your own judgement. You are lost. I will tell you where you need to go."

This was too much to take in for the weary catling. "Where, Mr Spirit? I felt so sure that we should leave the ship, but what if I made a mistake? I don't know where I am or how I got to this place."

"Fiåney has delivered you. Is that not enough?"

Mati frowned. He had wished for a greater explanation.

"You are needed," said the spirit. "I will guide you. When you rejoin your body, you will know what to do."

"Can I find you in Fiåney in case...?" In case *you* are needed, thought Mati.

"Do not rely on it. These are dangerous times. There are passages in Fiåney that even I dare not tread. The Great

Spirit's spies are everywhere, hunting down rebels."

Mati's fur bristled. "The Great Spirit?"

"Alia," whispered Obelghast. "It is dangerous to speak of her – even her name could conjure her presence."

Obelghast seemed wary – was he frightened for himself? Mati trembled, remembering what Bayo had said about the dream-wake: "You think they cannot make you bleed?" A mortal cat like Mati could be killed in Fiåney, his second self vanishing, leaving his body to perish. But a spirit wouldn't suffer a similar fate – isn't that what Bayo had told him? What exactly were his words? "You cannot kill what does not live."

"Are you in danger?" ventured Mati. "I thought it wasn't possible to—" his voice dropped— "to harm a spirit."

Obelghast seemed surprised. "There are things worse than death."

"Worse?"

"Is it not worse to be enslaved? There are those who praise the ancient tribes, the vital bloodlines. Yet are we not all noble? What are we, Mati, after all?"

The Tygrine was silent, and the spirit continued.

"We are cats. We are instinct, judgement and spirit. We were all born of Te Bubas, born to roam free. Shackle or cage us, no one can own us, for we are wild at heart."

Mati felt his fur tingle and a strange sensation of warmth swelled inside him. In that moment, he was no longer alone – he was part of something special – part of a race of creatures that were prouder, older, freer than all other beings.

The spirit spoke again. "Return now to the physical realm. Go swiftly and abandon your misgivings."

Mati sighed. Doubt gnawed at his soul. Why had he brought the catlings here? As he floated through Fiåney into wakefulness, the vision of the hilltop faded. He passed through darkness before breaking from his trance, and in that moment he thought he saw the moon flash like a white eye in the night. He returned to his body with a spasm of terror, shivering before his friends in the midday heat.

Jess's eyes were wide. "What is it, Mati?"

He started to answer but hesitated. On a sudden, irresistible impulse, he spun round. "We chase the sun," he said decisively. "Follow me!"

The catlings walked all afternoon along the edges of the city sprawl that gave way to voluptuous sand dunes. They trod awkwardly, paws sinking, springing from one step to another in clouds of dust. Sand clung beneath their paw pads, hung on their fur and settled on their whiskers. Mati strode ahead with purpose, an unerring certainty in his gait, and the others did not question him.

Light glanced off the grains of sand, dazzling their eyes. The young cats struggled deeper into the desert, following the sun as it slowly sank towards the dunes. They passed no others on their journey, no evidence of humans or their roads and buildings. No signposts in the sand.

The desperate heat began to wane but still the sweeping dunes sprawled infinitely. The catlings' shadows danced behind them as the afternoon rolled on, and with it the sky took on a hazy pinkness.

At last Jess spoke. "We can't... Mati, we can't go on without a break – without food or water." Her ear twitched involuntarily, disturbed by the sand. "You haven't told us where we're going – you haven't told us *anything*."

"Soon," said Mati vaguely. Although he was with her in the physical realm, there was distance in his eyes. Watching him, Jess could not find the words to break through to the catling she knew, to try to persuade him. Pangur wasn't there with his authoritative voice. There was no one to compel Mati or reason with him. Jess watched as the Tygrine turned away from her, springing over the sand once more. She followed, defeated, throwing Domino a quizzical look.

The sun dipped beneath the horizon in a shroud of violet. The temperature plummeted and Mati finally stopped. Gathered close to each other, the catlings washed their sandy fur.

Domino sneezed, sand tickling his nose. "This is hopeless!" he complained. "Why even try to get clean? We're surrounded by the stuff – we'll only be covered again before we know it."

"Strange to think that it all started in a desert like this one," said Mati absently.

Domino paused to look at him. "What started?"

"Life. Life started in the desert. The first cat, Te Bubas, told me." He paused, realizing that this was an insight from Fiâney. He rarely spoke about what he'd seen there. His friends were staring at him. "The earliest cats would have lived somewhere like this." He thought a moment. "Somewhere like this, but on a riverbank."

"Like Cressida Lock?" said Domino with longing.

Jess frowned. "That's hardly in a desert."

"Why would cats choose to live in a desert?" asked the harlequin catling. "It's so ... *uncomfortable*. So dry and hot in the day, and the sand's impossible. There doesn't seem to be any food around. It's freezing when the sun goes down and there's no shelter. Mati, are you sure cats lived around here? We haven't passed one since we entered the desert. We haven't passed *anything*."

Mati raised his back leg and spoke between washes. "I know it sounds strange, but it's true. There were cats in the desert, long ago. They lived without hinds. Not strays, not ferals but totally wild."

"That's what my hind told me," said Jess. "The Abyssinia Tygrine and cats of the Sa Mau."

Mati nodded, avoiding her gaze.

The catlings slept until awoken by discomfort. A confetti of stars lit the sky and the gibbous moon was white as milk.

"We should keep going," said Mati. His mouth was

245

parched and he swallowed. He had to get them out of this place. He didn't know where he was leading them – he only sensed the direction with a certainty that it was right. It tugged at his paws.

Unwillingly, his friends rose and followed. Nightfall had trailed its icy touch over the desert, with a wind that raised the sand to slap their fur. Jadedly, they trudged against it. The land seemed to sweep uphill in a difficult incline.

"I wonder how far we've travelled since leaving Cressida Lock," mused Domino, trying to be cheerful, despite everything. "I bet you anything we've gone further than most cats. Maybe further than *any* cat!"

"Maybe," said Mati distantly.

Far away from the bright lights of cities it was dark in the desert. Mati looked distrustfully at the moon. It seemed to urge him to go north, to deter him from his course. He lowered his eyes, recalling the spirit Obelghast and the impulse to push west. Moving in that direction he felt the world grow sweeter. Even the air seemed to welcome him, becoming warmer and strangely familiar.

By the first glimmer of dawn, the catlings could scarcely walk. Their throats were dry and their legs throbbed with weariness. Faltering feline steps had lapsed into a dazed stagger. Mati was several tail-lengths ahead, rarely glancing back at Jess and Domino.

I must go further, he thought. His pulse rushed in his temples, like the ancient river he had known as a kitten. For a moment he lost his sense of direction, longing this time to wander south. He frowned, struggling to focus. He was so drained that thoughts scarcely formed in his mind. *I must—*

Another step and his mouth fell open. Without realizing it, they had been mounting a hilltop. In the faint light he could see the silhouette of a mound of rocks and down below a steep descent into a valley. His head was spinning.

Here was the site where the Tygrine fought the Sa in the first great battle. Here was the place where the Tygrine fell.

With a pang of yearning, he started towards the rocks.

"Behind you, Mati!" It was Jess's voice, cracked and desperate.

Dizzily, he wheeled around. She and Domino were lower on the incline and blocking them, closing around Mati, were three huge cats. He could make out the fluid contour of their limbs, rippling with muscles. Large pointed ears framed their faces; fierce eyes flashed golden in the moonlight.

One of the cats took a step towards him. "Get away from the rocks! Who dares to cross the Tygrine Pinnacle? Speak now or die!"

Mati blinked at the cat. His sight was blurring, the features before him drifting in and out of clarity. He tried to find his tongue but exhaustion sluiced over him. His paws felt numb, trembling beneath him. "The hilltop," he murmured. "I have seen this place."

"Impossible! None but our kin has trodden this soil in ten thousand ages of the moon."

247

"I have seen it," repeated Mati in a voice as light as a breeze. "I have seen it in Fiåney." Again, his eyes misted, a storm of colour obscuring his vision. Then his head bowed and he sank: into sand; into dust; into darkness.

Ra'ha

Mati glided through the halls of Fiâney, a world of unlimited space. He felt no surprise when he arrived at the junction of the three passageways. He stepped away from the right passage, the Harakar, where tendrils of smoke escaped to circle the dreary air and pitiful mewls mingled with the bitter smell of ash.

In contrast, the middle passageway was silent. As Mati took a step towards the gateway to Sienta, he could feel his pulse slow down and the air grow still. He paused at the entrance for some time, blinking towards the gentle haze that hung impossibly in the distance. With an effort he pulled his face away, took a few steps back and turned to the third passageway.

He ran his tongue over his muzzle. The entrance was dark, revealing nothing of what lay beyond. Reaching through Fiåney he sensed no passing spirits. His instincts were quiet.

Is it wise to take a chance? wondered Mati. Without instinct, there could be no judgement. He turned away.

Sunlight exploded before Mati's eyes. He struggled to his feet, still woozy. Jess and Domino were by his side, worry ageing their young faces. The sun was already high overhead, and with it the blistering heat.

"You are awake, My Lord Mati."

Mati turned to see the large tom who had challenged him on arrival at the hilltop. The tom had tabby stripes running through his short fur and one of his ears was black. But his eyes were golden, like Mati's own, and the catling watched him with fascination. A few paces behind stood a number of other cats. Mati noticed that all of them had long limbs and large ears, much like himself, but in each case this was mixed with other features; splodges of tabby or white; green eyes instead of amber; bushy tails or feathery flanks.

Another cat came forward, a queen with a long, russet coat and a dead bird clasped in her jaws. She set it down before Mati and stepped back. "Come in peace," she murmured, catching his eye.

"We were told that you would appear, although we scarcely dared believe it," said the black-eared tom.

Mati cleared his throat. "Who are you?"

The tom's golden eyes twinkled. "The offering is made to you by Nalita, Principal Huntress and my consort in this small realm. My name is Lurian. I am Commander in Chief of the Army of the Abyssinia Tygrine – whatever is left of it. I was your amma's faithful servant."

Mati's heart ached at the mention of his mother. "She saw me to the ship."

"She was the most courageous *felis* I have ever known," said the Commander, "the bravest of her time, perhaps of all times. We came with her as far as the Tygrine Pinnacle, the shaft of rock overhanging the valley. It is the ancient crossing between the territories of Tygrine and Sa. She ordered us to remain. Here on the hilltop, we are safe. Down in the valley is *his* land, although he is yet to claim it. I do believe he dares not come. The Queen, your amma, cast a spell of protection over us, over the hilltop and back some way to the east. It exists through you. The Army of the Sa Mau cannot cross the Boundary – neither can their agents, allies or spies. No living cat may pass it unless their heart is faithful to the Tygrine cause."

Mati cast his eyes towards the rock mound near the edge of the Tygrine Pinnacle and beyond it to the valley below. "This is your territory?" It wasn't where he'd been raised by his mother – of that he felt sure. He longed for that place with the winding river, the rustling reeds and the chirp of cicadas.

"Our ancient homeland is further south. My Lord, it is

251

so beautiful. A lush place of waterfalls, delicious fish and sheltering trees." Lurian's eyes clouded a moment as he drifted through his memories. "We cannot return there. The road is thick with traitors and spies. Members of our tribe left to rebuild the old land. They did not get far. One escaped and told of an ambush."

Mati frowned. From the cats around him he sensed a swell of bitter sadness. It crackled in the midday sun. Some, he knew, were recalling their fallen kin. Faces danced before Mati's eyes and a jolt of yearning passed through him, a pain so vivid that he winced.

Lurian's face darkened, his one black ear flicking back in agitation. "We still live independently of hinds; we are far from their cruelty and control. We can rove south for a stretch over the desert; have located streams where the water is sweet. Among us are expert hunters and we never go hungry. But we are as good as prisoners, bound to the land around the hilltop for fear of the Suzerain's treachery."

Several of the cats growled at this, tails swishing with anger.

Lurian continued. "The Queen sensed that despite her spell, you would not be safe in this land. The Suzerain would never cease to stalk her: be it through this world or the dream-wake, she feared that he would find her in the end. You were her secret, the object of her passion and her love. The Suzerain knew nothing of your birth and the Queen believed that this alone would save you.

252

"The night that the Queen sent you away was the darkest we have suffered. For we knew she went to certain death and feared you too would perish. I begged to go with her – a life without the Queen could scarcely be worth living. She refused. 'Wait at the Tygrine Pinnacle, Lurian,' she said. 'For my son shall arrive one day to reclaim his territory. He will need you to aid him. As you served me, you shall serve him.'"

Mati glanced around, taking in the faces of the watching cats. "You are the Tygrines, my mother's allies?"

"My Lord, we are but what is left of them. For the Suzerain's army is brutal beyond reckoning. He has driven us from our ancient quarters, rounded us up and felled us like the papyrus flowers that grow along the Nile. The Tygrines have no might to defeat him. What once was an army of princes has been diminished beyond recognition through bitter ages of conflict. Our blood has been diluted. You, My Lord, alone are true – you are the last pure-blooded descendant of the Tygrine line."

These words were greeted with silence from the surrounding cats, who watched Mati with a powerful intensity.

"We have waited many moons," said Lurian. "We feared you would never come."

Mati's whiskers twitched at the mention of the moon. It still taunted him, despite the fall of the phantom.

The Commander did not seem to notice. "I scarcely

253

believed it when I saw you arrive – a catling with two kinless strays. Forgive me my boldness for I knew not who you were. I feared the lure of the rocks."

Mati watched him. "What do you mean?"

One of the tribe gave an involuntary miaow that Lurian silenced with a look. He turned back to Mati, running his eyes over Jess and Domino. For a moment he paused, distracted by the red collar around the young queen's neck. "Be wary of the rocks, My Lord. They circle a chasm – a gap within the fabric of the earth that has been there since the dawn of time. Powerful energy escapes it, invisible to the eye. That is how your amma, both warrior and sage, was able to cast here a spell of protection. She with such wisdom dared approach it while shalians and soothsayers fell to their doom. The rock circle is perilous and I beg you to keep clear."

Mati's eyes widened. "Where does the ... the chasm lead?"

Lurian held his gaze. "It does not lead anywhere."

Mati's fur prickled. "But if you fell?"

"Why, you would fall for eternity."

Jess took a step towards Mati and the three catlings gazed in horror at the rock mound.

The Commander spoke again. "You are quite safe, provided that you do not venture near. But be wary. The rocks have a powerful pull – they may call you to them, hungering for a sacrifice."

"I almost…" Mati's words faded. Lurian was right – hadn't he been drawn to the rock mound, compelled to approach it? He wanted the Commander to tell him more but the black-eared tom was already changing the subject.

"Only a cat of your lineage would have ventured into Fiåney and discovered this lonely hilltop. To have found it in this realm, none other could have done. And when I looked upon you I knew – I knew I was in the presence of majesty."

Lurian sat in front of Mati, blinking his eyes in a gesture of friendship. "Come in peace, My Lord. I was loyal to your amma till the end, and such allegiance I now offer you."

Mati turned to Jess and Domino. "I couldn't have made it here without my friends." At this, he felt the tribe tense, glancing at Lurian curiously. He sensed that he was asking a lot of them – that they were proud of their claims to the Tygrine line, distrustful of strangers from the outside world.

Lurian nodded. "If these cats have aided you they are most welcome. They shall know Tygrine hospitality and need fear nothing of us. We bid you all to eat well and rest – for with your arrival we are stronger – we are fit to be kings once more!"

Mati stared at the Commander. Within the tom's golden eyes he saw a lifetime of suffering, of battle and defeat. This cat had loved and lost his dearest friends; he had grown hard from his sorrows. Yet deep within him burned a flame

255

of hope. He longed to serve – to repay the kindnesses of Mati's mother – to prove himself a warrior true to the Tygrine tribe.

Mati blinked back at Lurian and felt the Commander's gratitude. He looked in turn to the assembled cats and met the gaze of each, one after the other.

When he broke away, Lurian rose to his paws. "Tonight there shall be a feast fit for the ancient Lords, for the King has claimed his title! Victory to the Abyssinia Tygrine! We are united once more!"

A flock of desert larks took to the air as the Tygrines broke into an explosion of miaows and *pirrups*.

"The King is home!" they cried. "Long live the Tygrine cat!"

After Mati, Jess and Domino had eaten a light meal, Nalita, the long-furred russet queen, led them down the sweeping hilltop, away from the valley. They passed Tygrine fighters on the way. The cats were tall, like Mati, but years of surviving in the desert had conditioned them. Their faces were angular, without the remains of Mati's kitten-fat, and their muscular limbs exuded power. They sat still and alert as the catlings passed, eyes narrowed in respect.

Nalita brought them to a collection of craggy rocks, around which curled a narrow stream. "Drink," she said. "It is quite safe."

The catlings dipped their heads and lapped heartily,

delighting in the clear, sweet water. Once they had drunk their fill, Nalita moved on and they followed.

Eventually the land stopped curving downhill and the sand stretched flat and featureless before them. Two large boulders stood in the sand and here Nalita paused. "Not twenty paces on is the Boundary, the border of our territory. Do not pass it. The spell of protection cannot reach you out there."

Domino gulped fearfully. He sniffed the air, trying to make out a territorial imprint, like the scent of a chief. His eyes searched for some kind of barrier – a signpost to tell him where the dangerous land began. "But how will we know? How can we be sure we won't cross it?" he blurted out worriedly.

"Why have we stopped so close to it when it's invisible?" Jess put in. "We can't smell anything."

Mati turned to his friends. "Don't you feel it?" To Mati, the contours of the Boundary were as sharp and clear as if someone had built a fence around them. A powerful essence floated around him, something rich and sweet that recalled within him, with an unceasing ache, his first days at his mother's side. Stretching out his senses he felt the Boundary grow thin. Every instinct warned him to stay within it. It was more than self-protection, he realized. It made him feel closer to his mother.

Nalita glanced momentarily at Domino. "We do not normally accept visitors from outside the tribe – and we do not expect to see them so deep in the desert. You may not feel it at once but soon it will be part of you. The lines of the Boundary will become as clear as any tom's scent. Clearer. Your master has no trouble, for he is a Tygrine. What he knows of instinct, you shall learn."

Mati caught his breath. She had referred to him as their master – his friends would not like that. He could sense Jess bridle at the comment, and Domino dip his head, feeling foolish.

Nalita continued. "I have brought you here, so close to the Boundary, because it is the furthest point in our territory from the rock mound. It is best to avoid being anywhere near it until you are accustomed to its call, and can resist it. Here along the Boundary none can touch you and you may rest without fear of harm." She led them to a shaded cavern between the boulders. The tan feathers of a nightjar had been laid over the sandy floor. It was like a cave, smaller than the chambers in the catacombs but cool and comfortable. Tygrine fighters were posted nearby, eager to protect their king.

Nalita bid them farewell. She would return when the moon was at its highest point. There would be a feast in Mati's honour. "O auspicious night," she said. "For it is a full moon."

"We used to meet on a full moon too," said Domino.

"We?" The queen looked at him doubtfully.

"My kin – the Cressida Cats. We met beneath the full moon. Funny that we have the same habits when everything

258

else is so *different*."

"Funny?" Nalita stared at him coolly. "You are still some sort of cat, are you not? This is no coincidence. The moon is a powerful lord. Its eye watches the night. By its grace, we hunt; by its treachery, we fight and fall. You may not know it, catling, but the moon compelled the meeting of your kin – not the other way around. The moon when full is at its most powerful – for only then can it rival the sun."

Domino didn't reply, mouth parted in wonder at what Nalita said. But next to him, Mati miaowed nervously. The moon still scared him. He feared its allegiances. He sensed its dark purpose.

Nalita left them alone in the cavern between the boulders. For a while, the catlings sat in silence. Domino stared at Mati, wide-eyed, his awe for his friend restored by what he had heard from Lurian and the reverence paid Mati by the Tygrine tribe.

Mati's serious face grew mischievous and he pirruped. "You needn't look at me like that. I haven't grown two heads!" On impulse he nipped his black-and-white friend on the ear.

"Scarcely behaviour fitting a king!" scoffed Domino, glancing towards the entrance of the cavern. The Tygrine fighters were out of earshot.

"Good!" declared Mati.

Jess watched him, a playful twitch to her tail. "I am just pleased to see the old Mati back."

259

Mati turned to her, shoving her gently with a russet paw. "He never went away, not really!"

The three catlings fought and capered amiably, sand clinging to their fur. They collapsed against each other, purring. Soon they were fast asleep, a contented mass of russet, tortoiseshell and white.

Through long passages of sleep, Mati's world was a swirling fog. Then he trailed into a dream where moonlight filled the sky. He heard the lonely *kroo-kroo-kroo!* of a nightjar and the faintest gasp of water through a stream. The moon pulsed white and a silent army gathered in a darkened valley. Then the sound of movement over sand: not the light, fluid footfall of a cat but something jerky, dragging.

He escaped the boundaries of this dream into Fiåney, the limitless labyrinth that wove between dreams. The white moon vanished and the call of the nightjar faded. Still he could hear the murmur of water and he started towards it without thought or intention. Briefly he passed through the point where three passageways met, and in the indigo light he took the last one, to his left. The dream-wake darkened, deepest black, but he continued without pause, trusting himself to instinct. Steadily, the babble of water grew louder. A gentle light gathered in the distance and a warm wind played with his fur. The land before him was emerald green and, looking down, he saw grass beneath his paws. The air was woody, a hint of pine and cedar, crisp and damp like the first breath of dawn in a meadow. Birds twittered cheerfully and a rainbow hummed on the horizon. The sun was bright but the heat mild and Mati was aware of an intense feeling of comfort. He found a spot by a burst of cornflowers where he sat and washed his face.

He lowered his moistened paw with a surge of excitement. He was not alone. He blinked. In the distance, weaving through the long grass, was a tomcat. Mati's eyes became saucers, watching as the tom came closer. His fur was jet black, shimmering in the sunlight. His green eyes sparkled.

Mati rose to his paws. "Mr Pangur?" He took a step towards him, jaws gaping in disbelief.

The tom's tail swished playfully. "I've told you before, it's just Pangur!"

"It is you!" The catling sprang towards the tomcat, leaping over the lush grass. He made to rub his face against that rich black fur but felt nothing. *No touch in the dream-wake.* He stepped back.

"So you made it here at last."

"But where—?"

The tomcat purred. "This is Ra'ha."

Mati gazed at him in wonder, recalling what Te Bubas had said: "The paths of the dream-wake are limitless. There are pastures in Fiåney where the grass grows thick and the sun shines in eternal summer. None can age and no one dies. It is the land of memory, and within it our fallen friends shall live for ever."

"I am so sorry, Pangur..." said Mati. "I did nothing, I panicked, I—"

"None of your nonsense, catling. You have seen me now. You know that there is nothing to be scared of in this land. It is you for whom I fear, for your burden is a great one. If I have eased it in some small way, then let us call it a privilege. Foolishly I have questioned you in the past. Perhaps I was too quick to bend to the idle doubts of others; perhaps what you told me was too difficult to hear – and if so, I reproach myself as a coward."

"How can you say that? You're the bravest cat I've ever met!"

As Mati was speaking, another cat emerged from the grasses, he too with charcoal fur and bright green eyes.

Pangur glanced back. "My brother, Hanratty. We have seen our amma too!"

"Your amma?" Mati's heart jumped in hope. For if Pangur and Hanratty had seen their mother, perhaps Mati might meet his own in this magical place?

"She is here," said Pangur, eyeing him knowingly. "Your amma. She is here if you will it."

"What do you mean?" asked Mati.

Hanratty spoke. "This is the land of memory beyond the third gate. *Your memory*. If you remember her, so she shall come to you."

"But I do remember!" Mati's eyes widened. He thought with longing of her beautiful face, her black-rimmed eyes and her

262

sonorous voice. Craning his neck he stared beyond the toms where the grasses rolled towards a forest of ancient trees.

"Then go to her, Mati."

The catling glanced at Pangur. "I miss you, sir."

"I am always here, as long as your heart desires it." He blinked at Mati and lowered his head. "Now go."

Mati nodded, already pacing towards the forest. He trembled with excitement. He longed to see his mother so much that it hurt him to think of it and for a moment he paused, unsure what he'd do if he did not find her.

The grass before him danced on the breeze, ducking and weaving in pools of shadow cast by trees.

"Mati?" She was behind him, framed in sunlight. "My child," she purred. "My dear kit."

He lowered his face. "Amma…" He struggled for words. "I've missed you so much! Where have you been?"

She blinked at him. Her voice was low. "I have not *been*. I only observe. Your departure from Cressida Lock; how you rescued Pritin's kits."

"You know!"

"I see it all. Fiåney knows, and I am a part of it now. I am part of memory."

He took a step towards her. He would have given everything to touch her then, to nuzzle her neck and feel her fur.

"Amma, I can't believe it – you're alive!"

"Alive in Ra'ha, as long as you remember me. Never forget me, child."

263

"Never," said Mati. "Not now that I've found you. It's been such a long journey."

"But you were not alone."

Mati felt warmed at the thought of Jess and Domino, and the others who had helped him on his way. "No, I wasn't alone. Although I often feel lonely." He raised his face and gazed into his mother's golden eyes. "Why is that, Amma?"

"Every cat walks their own path," she said simply. "It is the burden of our kind – that we are independent. And yours is the greater, for you alone carry the Tygrine legacy."

He nodded. Her words had recalled to him the spirit Obelghast.

Mati uttered aloud, "We are cats. We are instinct, judgement and spirit. We were all born of Te Bubas, born to roam free. Shackle or cage us, no one can own us, for we are wild at heart."

His mother stared at him. "Who told you that?"

"A spirit, Amma. A spirit called—"

She cut him off. "It does not matter. It is safer not to speak his name."

"Safer?" Mati's hairs rose along his neck. "Are we still in danger, even here? Even in Ra'ha?"

His mother blinked at him with sadness and love. "The lord of the Sa Mau would not agree with the words you have spoken. He believes only in the majesty of his tribe, and in his own authority. I have heard him, Mati. 'One law', he says."

Mati shivered. "It isn't over, is it?" he asked.

The Tygrine Queen did not answer. The brightness of her eyes faded, and the air around them dimmed, as though someone had snuffed out a candle. A sharp wind rose from deeper in the forest, rustling the leaves on the ancient trees. Mati heard a dragging sound and glancing behind him he saw a distant fleck of shadow, just beyond Ra'ha in Fiåney's dark Borderlands. It hovered in the sky, a swirling clot, like the hawks over the fallow field. When Mati turned back towards the meadow his mother had vanished. Before his eyes, the green pasture melted; the bushy trees grew straight and rigid, their leaves shrinking into thorns. The temperature plummeted as around him unravelled a twilight world. Overhead the swirling clot drew nearer, fading into white, pulsing like the moon.

"Amma?" Mati whispered. The word echoed through the vaults of the dream-wake. She was gone; she was memory – a fragment of his own spirit; a piece of himself that he could never quite grasp.

For a moment he recalled the Borderlands of Fiåney and the shalian, Etheleldra. Her words came back to him, stunned him with all their terrible force: "Is it cruelty and hatred that can break your will – or is it love?"

Standing alone in the darkness of the dream-wake, Mati threw back his head and yowled in despair.

No Living Cat

A commotion outside woke the catlings with
a start. They could hear the growls of Tygrine
fighters, scent their fear fanning round them in wafts – and
yet they smelled no other presence on the night air. Mati
crept, fur raised, to the entrance of the cavern as Jess and
Domino stood behind him.

"Mati, don't!" begged Jess.

Domino peered over Mati's shoulder. "What is it?"

Mati couldn't answer. Fear clenched his throat and he
froze, watching as the Tygrines rounded on a jerking, shifting figure. They circled it in formation, backs arched, baring
their teeth. He could hardly see it beyond the shapes of the
fighters; a flash of green eyes; a snatch of sharp claws.

The phantom! It had survived. It had followed him.

This is the end, thought Mati. He almost longed for it,

recalling Ra'ha, the land of memory. With terrible anguish he had been torn from that place. All he wanted was to return there – to be with his mother. To stay in Ra'ha for ever.

Quick as a flash, Lurian the Commander had joined the circling fighters. "Thing of the Sa!" he growled with disgust. "Warped, repulsive distortion of cat! Scentless being of the Harakar! By what trickery did you enter our land?"

Then Mati realized that the phantom had crossed the lines of the Boundary into the Tygrine territory. It trembled and lashed its three faces in confusion, hissing and spitting with rage. Its rolling eyes scrutinized the fighters, searching.

Domino was by Mati's side. "It's *alive*! But how?"

"And it's inside the Boundary," Jess confirmed. "Didn't Lurian say that no one could enter unless – what was it? Unless their heart is 'faithful to the Tygrine cause'."

Lurian leapt at the phantom, throwing the creature to the ground as others closed in. It struggled with the Tygrine fighters as the catlings held their breath. The phantom resisted wildly but beneath their might, it stilled.

"Thank goodness," sighed Domino.

Slowly, the fighters fell back, wounded but triumphant. Mati took a step forward, front paw hovering uncertainly. Before him the phantom was slumped against the sand. The creature showed no injury of its own. Motionless it looked almost like three separate cats, something more familiar and less fearful. Suddenly, three sets of amber eyes flickered in one face. It clambered to its paws with a terrifying hiss. Once more it was a single, heaving mass.

"This cannot be," murmured Lurian. "We killed it! *This cannot be!*"

The phantom paid no attention to the Commander. Its lurching eyes had caught the outline of a catling at the entrance to the cavern between the boulders. It gave a long, rasping "hissssss".

"No!" cried Nalita. "We must protect Mati!"

"M-a-a-a-t-i," hissed the phantom. *"M-a-a-a-t-i."* Immediately the Tygrines closed around it again, blocking its path, pushing it back.

There's no point, thought Mati. It can't be stopped. He stood bolted to the sand, beneath the full moon. Fear ripped through him, his breath clawing at his lungs and hammering against his chest. In his mind's eye he sank in and out of Fiåney. Over the creature's hiss he heard the sound of rushing water, the call of a nightjar, the shriek of seagulls and voices of spirits.

He was only passingly aware of the commotion around him; of the fighters' efforts to thwart the phantom; of Jess's miaows of terror. Shards of Fiåney slashed through the barriers of the waking world. He heard the gravelly voice of Obelghast, the insistent calls of Bayo, but their words mingled and vanished in the vastness of the night.

Domino cowered at Mati's side. "Can't you kill him like you killed Mithos?"

His friend's voice hauled Mati back to his first self. The Tygrine fighters had retreated a few paces. One lay unmoving, blood seeping into the sand; others writhed helplessly from their wounds.

Once more, the phantom seemed slain. It lay almost peacefully, three languid bodies. Then, with sickening familiarity, its eyes shot open and it groped clumsily to its paws. Its shuddering faces turned immediately to Mati.

He stared back, too scared to speak or pull away. As he looked on, horrified, the phantom transformed from three beings into one. Its eyes roved against a shifting face. For an instant Mati caught its menacing gaze and sank into the pool of its thoughts. A mist of wrath engulfed him and he staggered, as though struck. As the mist parted, three separate stories unravelled before him; three kittens, born of a great queen and once revered by many. The kittens had russet fur, like his own, with wide-spaced ears and golden eyes. They had grown into fearless young cats, blessed with exceptional gifts. With time they might have each become shalians but their impatience led them to Fiåney, to long experiments in the feline dream-wake. Their mother had warned them about the dangers of that gloomy land. "Do not stray far, my children," she had entreated. But one warm evening they had dared each other to leave their bodies far behind; they roved deep into the dream-wake's labyrinths. They had grown lost.

Their mother was a noble cat, of high birth. She had

called in shalians to try to save them, she had protected their first selves with spells. But the young cats never returned. Eventually, their bodies perished but their spirits remained, drifting restlessly around the halls of the dream-wake, consumed with bitterness for the life they had left behind.

Mati finally spoke, his voice a murmur. "You were Tygrines once."

Even Jess and Domino, standing beside him, barely heard their friend's words. But the phantom's ears shot forward and it hissed with loathing: "T-y-y-g-rine."

Mati frowned, deep in thought. How had three spirits – once catlings of the Tygrine tribe – found their way out of Fiåney? What dark magic had led them from that realm?

He cleared his throat. "The Suzerain called you from the dream-wake, didn't he?"

"Su-u-u-zerain," hissed the phantom. "F-r-iend."

"He's the leader of the Sa, he's no friend of yours," said Mati, holding its gaze. "Don't you know who you are? He's mocking you – using you to destroy your own kind. You used to be Tygrines."

"T-y-y-g-rine not s-a-a-a-v-e us! Should s-a-a-a-v-e us!"

"You can't blame the Tygrine tribe for what happened to you – you strayed too deep into Fiåney. Your amma did everything she could."

The creature threw back its head and mewled desperately, a rasping, distorted sound. Mati ached, sharing its pain, despite everything. For the phantom – the three cats

270

it used to be – had become trapped in Fiåney, never ageing, as their mother grew old and perished in the waking world. Mati thought of his own mother. Her spirit still lingered in Fiåney, but it seemed he would always be parted from her: trapped in his body, destined to live a mortal life.

The Tygrine army watched, creeping closer to the creature, although none by now expected that they could defeat it. The phantom saw them and lunged, throwing off the fighters who leapt in its path.

Countless years in Fiåney had destroyed this being – the cats it once was. Mati had seen the truth of this in that momentary gaze: whatever it had been, this creature could not be reasoned with. Its desperate fury would never be quenched.

Mati turned and bolted out of the cavern and up the hilltop, skidding against the sand. He tried to summon energy from Fiåney. But the phantom was faster. It rounded ahead of Mati, blocking his way. Several of the Tygrine fighters appeared behind them, Lurian at the lead. The Commander pulled back on his haunches, about to pounce on the phantom once more. Blood poured from a wound across his cheek and one of his fangs had been snapped off in the previous tussle. A further struggle with the phantom would kill him.

"Commander, to the rocks!" Mati cried, catching Lurian with his golden eyes. They seemed to glow with a light of their own, dazzling in the darkness.

The Commander obeyed wordlessly, fleeing towards the rock mound.

Don't fall, thought Mati, go close, not too close! But there was no time to say more as Lurian vanished up the hill. Already the phantom was hurtling towards Mati.

"What is it you want?" Mati cried.

It hesitated, glaring at him. He knew it was a creature of Fiåney, a sort of broken spirit. By some sorcery it had escaped into the physical realm. Jess hadn't understood how it had passed the Boundary – a barrier that no living cat could cross, unless their heart was faithful to the Tygrine cause. *But this was no living cat.*

The phantom's body quaked with confusion and despair. "A-a-a-m-m-a! Su-u-u-zerain s-w-e-a-r!"

"The Suzerain can't promise to give you your amma!" Mati miaowed. "Don't you see? She died long ago. He can't summon her body from the dead – no one can. You will not find her in the world of the living. You will not find peace."

In the background appeared the Tygrine army, followed by Jess and Domino. Over the clamour, Mati again heard the nightjar and the rush of an invisible river.

"Kill T-y-y-g-rine! Kill M-a-a-a-t-i! Suz-e-rain f-r-iend! Suz-e-rain s-w-ear!" The creature floundered, uncertainty wrinkling its face, its paws beating the sand. Rage rose from it in poisonous waves, the surrounding air sharp with acidity. "A-a-a-m-m-a!"

Mati took his chance to tear around the phantom. He

knew instinctively what he had to do – had somehow known it all along. It was the phantom itself that had given him the answer. For the three young cats who had delved deep into Fiåney had never escaped. They had become prisoners of the dream-wake. Even as their bodies aged and decayed, their spirits had lingered in that parallel world.

The anguish of losing his mother had returned to Mati, raw and immediate. His loss drove him recklessly along a path he felt destined to follow. As he reached the hilltop, he saw with relief that Lurian was perched on the rocks. Below them gaped the valley, the site of ancient conflict between the Tygrine and the Sa. Power surged from the rock mound, the same dangerous force that had beckoned Mati to this place. A force that Mati knew all too well. Feeling the phantom at his tail, he bounded up the rocks.

Lurian's eyes widened. "My Lord, no! Not that! Please, My Lord! Let us kill it – we will find a way!"

The words of the spirit Bayo leapt to Mati's tongue: "You cannot kill a phantom. You cannot kill what does not live." Mati flew up the mound, his paws scarcely skimming the rocks. "Catch me!" he ordered and leapt into the abyss, the phantom at his heels.

The panic-ridden Commander sprang over the mouth of the chasm, seizing the catling by the scruff and hauling him onto the hilltop. Lurian's fur singed as the phantom flew past him and tumbled into darkness. The fighters converged on the hilltop as the wounded Commander set Mati down.

"What has happened to him?" whimpered Nalita, arriving with the rest of the Tygrines.

The Commander nudged the limp catling with a paw. "It is nothing, just a faint."

Jess pushed through the throng of Tygrines. "His eyes!" she cried.

The cats stared at Mati. His eyes were wide open, their golden light extinguished.

Jess collapsed at his side, overcome with grief. "This is no faint! Don't you see what he's done? To trap the phantom, he has led it to the chasm. His body is here, but his spirit has gone – he is lost to us for ever!"

Into darkness they plunged, the phantom and the spirit of the Tygrine cat. They thrashed in the air amid powerful currents that sucked them deeper, spinning and sinking as though through a whirlpool. The world around them was black. Nothing emerged in the darkness; no fear or hatred, no love nor light.

Muddled thoughts consoled Mati's spirit as he spun through the dream-wake. For he knew that the chasm led to three gates at Fiåney's mysterious heart. Within Fiåney, he would rediscover Ra'ha. He would track down his mother. He would find eternal peace.

Silence gave way to a murmur of voices, which rose softly around him. The words mingled and crashed over him, both friendly and hostile. Some seemed to be offering him warnings, or advice. Others spoke across him, perhaps indifferent to his plight – unaware that they were overhead.

"A ghost – a phantom... You cannot kill what does not live..."

"Nature forbids what you seek. The world of the spirits and that of blood are separate domains..."

"You have a gift, and all gifts come with responsibilities..."

"Is it cruelty and hatred that can break your will – or is it love?"

"Damn the tribes to eternal war...!"

Deeper he fell, instinctively bracing his paws beneath him. Jess's face appeared to him, her green eyes brilliant against the patchwork of her fur. "I've missed you too, old friend..."

He reached out to her but she faded into darkness. Instead, he sensed the presence of the phantom, lashing the air, groping towards him with its many hooked claws.

Ra'ha, thought Mati: I must return to Ra'ha. As this thought took shape in his mind, so the air appeared to lighten and the space around him developed a green tinge. He could smell earth and grass and hear the twitter of birds. Heart leaping with joy, he knew that he was almost there – almost at the gate to Ra'ha, the land of memory. Soon he could stop and rest until the end of time.

The misty green grew more distinct. As Mati plunged, he could see the shape of forest trees and taste the meadow dew upon his tongue. Now is the time, he thought. If I wish to stay in Ra'ha, I must do something. I must do something to put an end to this fall. His mind strained with concentration. He sensed his descent begin to slow. He was in control! He could halt time with the force of his will. He would compel it to stop where his memory was at its sharpest.

Mati's heart thumped with excitement. Amma, I'm almost there! Wait for me!

A ghoulish hiss disturbed this reverie, reminding him of the ever-present phantom overhead. If Mati passed the third gate into Ra'ha, the creature would surely follow him. What damage would it do to his memories there? What evil would it wreak? And how would he ever be rid of it? Hurtling through Fiåney, he and the phantom were locked together. Undead – unkillable – destined to haunt each other until the end of time.

The green pasture that surrounded them grew fainter. Mati strained to see it – to smell its earthiness and hear birdsong. Doubt distorted his senses.

"Amma?" he called but the dream-wake was silent. Even in his memory, he could not see her face.

The borders of Ra'ha rushed out of view and the landscape grew black and featureless. Mati was in freefall again. His heart was numb. Ra'ha had passed out of reach: there was nothing worth fighting for any more.

A single voice emerged from the darkness. It was the

voice of Te Bubas: "The earth was forged by the will of the Creators. The same will that made me... To have is to lose, the earth was soon to learn. And so I too learned." Her words were rich with gentle authority and he felt that they shared the same plight. Mati sensed the phantom tremble above him. It moaned and bucked. Some ancient instinct led it to understand Te Bubas. It too was sharing in her journey.

Glistering stars appeared in the darkness. Their lurching descent seemed to slow again as a red dawn broke over a desert. The earth was parched, devoid of life, and all around them stretched sand dunes. Soon it didn't feel as though they were moving at all. The desert expanded into the distance, where every grain of sand was a separate fragment of the feline soul.

The phantom inched closer, its twisted paw pads almost clasping Mati's tail. Fury bubbled on its mouth. Perhaps it had realized that the Suzerain's promise would never be kept. Perhaps deep down it knew that its mother was gone for ever: that no one could bring her back. It no longer remembered the three cats it once was. No images remained in its mind of the kittenhood they had shared. It had nothing left but its anger – the inextinguishable desire to destroy.

Not here, thought Mati. Not in Sienta. Better to fall than be trapped with the phantom in this silent land.

The desert darkened and on they tumbled, down through endless night. What will become of me? Mati wondered.

His thoughts were disturbed by murmurings from the dream-wake. He heard voices rising in unison, too soft to emerge as words. Time passed incalculably: a heartbeat, an age of the sun.

At last the murmurs formed haunting chants:

Those who know the Tygrine's secret
Those who feel the Sa Mau's hate
We bid entry to our kingdom
No more centuries to wait...
We shall guide you to the gate

The gate. The first gate: the darkest and most terrible. A place of evil, where the Suzerain drew his sinister powers. Mati would sooner drift through Fiåney for eternity than spend a single second in the Harakar. *The Harakar.* A word unfamiliar to ordinary cats. A farm cat would not know it; a street cat could not think of it. But someone had uttered it, outside the dream-wake. Mati remembered. It was Lurian's horrified exclamation on sighting the phantom: "Warped, repulsive distortion of cat! Scentless being of the Harakar!"

As these words returned to Mati, the chanting voices of the high priests grew louder.

Those who wander endlessly
Those whose eyes no longer see
Ha'atta, ha'atta...

* * *

The air grew misty with a bitter taste as the distant crackle of flames burst along invisible corridors. Piteous whines rose over the voices of the priests and a long, foreboding cackle echoed through the air. Here was the gateway to the dungeons of the dream-wake.

Again Jess's face sprang before his eyes and with it a desperate impulse to return to his own world – to the land of the first self. He had fallen through Ra'ha. He had passed Sienta. This was his last chance to escape before launching into eternity.

Steeling himself against pain and terror, Mati focused his mind. As soon as they began to slow down, the phantom lunged. It caught Mati's second self with an outstretched paw, five jagged claws raking his body. Mati twisted out of its reach and leapt into a cloud of smoke. His paws touched solid ground and he sprang blindly ahead, the phantom close behind him and gaining by the moment.

Mati zigzagged through the mazes of the Harakar. There has to be a way out, he thought urgently. I got out before – I can do it again.

Liquid gushed over his paws and he stumbled on, crashing into smouldering walls, brittle as broken teeth.

The hawks! thought Mati. They crossed the boundary between the spirit and physical realms – that's how I escaped the Harakar. But the hawks are dead, the gate is closed. *I'm trapped!*

The phantom was close now, hissing with three voices, excited as a wolf sensing its quarry.

"I can't win!" cried Mati. "It is *his* place! I was a fool to come back here!"

"Have you learned so little on your journeys into Fiåney?"

Mati gasped, heady with relief, "Bayo, sir, is that really you?"

"The Cat Lord is coming!" said the spirit. "He knows you are here."

"He has tricked me – lured me back!"

"But it is *not* his place alone. You are of the same ancient legacy. It is your place too, to exploit as you will."

Mati bounded over scorching water, scarcely able to think. Hot wind blew in his face and he drove against it. "You said that the Cat Lord is coming," he whimpered. "All is lost…"

"Great Spirit Alia watched you pass through the second and third gates. She knew you would return here, by some curious compulsion that only she can understand. She whispered this to the Cat Lord – and now he is expecting you. He means to surprise you – but perhaps the surprise shall be his."

"I don't understand."

"Then do not try. Take courage: run faster. Run straight and true. Trust to the power of the dream-wake and leave your fears behind you!"

Mati breathed deeply, driving harder through the

Harakar, focusing on Bayo's words. He tried to push aside the haunting yowls and screams. The voices of chanting priests grew louder, deafening, rolling into a clash of thunder – shaking the walls of the Harakar – announcing the arrival of the Suzerain.

The silhouette of a spotted cat danced before Mati's eyes. *It's him! He's here!* Mati realized with horror. He was racing too fast to stop and he leapt at the Cat Lord without thought, diving through the translucent shape just before it solidified, bursting out of the other side into a bolt of light.

Mati glanced back. Within the dazzling brightness he glimpsed a tunnel, and at its entrance a jagged gateway where the Suzerain stood in a cloud of smoke. Then the tunnel disappeared and a blinding light enclosed Mati, so sharp he shut his eyes.

Beyond the first gate, in the land called the Harakar, the Cat Lord gasped. Something had punched through him and he staggered.

"My Lord, beware!" It was Great Spirit Alia, shrieking her alarm.

The Suzerain spun around. Flames leapt in the distance, plumes of smoke filling the gloomy chamber. For a moment it obscured his view and he sniffed the air. Was someone near? He could not smell anything unexpected – just the usual fumes of fire and ash. The smoke ebbed. From it emerged a jerking, heaving shape. Once it was three young cats, curious and hungry for adventure: they had explored the depths of Fiåney, against their mother's wishes. They had grown lost and their spirits had lingered there, long after their first selves perished. Untold ages in the dream-wake's dark corridors had darkened their hearts. A promise of a final reunion had roused them from Fiåney, had seen them released to the world not as three young cats but as a single, malformed being: decayed beyond recognition, bent on destruction.

The Suzerain's jaw fell. Ipanel had warned him that nature would seek its revenge. Yet he had never imagined that it would come like this – that he would be meeting his monster face to face beyond a gateway he claimed as his own.

Three sets of flickering eyes rested on the Suzerain. The phantom mewled then – a terrible, piteous sound: "You s-w-ear! *You lie!*" It pounced at the Cat Lord.

"Forgive me, Lamet!" The Suzerain screamed as the smoke closed in.

Mati opened his eyes. A familiar face looked down at him. He smelled the sweetness of her fur; felt the warmth of her gaze. She leaned over and washed his face. Beyond her, the sky was dark, powdered with infinite stars. Huddled among them, watching over the night, hovered the luminous moon.

"Welcome back, Mati," she purred quietly.

"Jess." His voice was husky – scarcely his own. He blinked

and raised his head. Domino, Lurian and Nalita were standing nearby, their faces alive with relief. Beyond them stood the army of the Abyssinia Tygrine.

Lurian stepped forward. "My Lord, you fell through the rocks. No cat has ever split their body – left it at the foot of the physical realm – while offering their spirit to that dark abyss. No one has ever fallen through it and returned." He dipped his head. Raising it again, he caught the glow in Mati's eyes and faltered. Perhaps he remembered the eyes of his old mistress, the Tygrine Queen. He cleared his throat. "We lost you for a day and night where the moon glowed red and the sun scarcely rose beyond a wall of mist. Where did you go to, My Lord? What did you see as you fell through the chasm?"

The Tygrine cats drew nearer and they listened with their whiskers pressed forward, hanging onto every word.

"I visited a land of fire, a place of chaos and despair; I saw the ancient world where the first cat was born; I even passed a meadow where our fallen friends remain. They wander there eternally, in safety and in peace. It may sound strange but this restful place was almost my undoing."

Lurian's eyes widened. Then he nodded. "My Lord, a feast of celebration shall be enjoyed in your name. Will you eat?"

"A feast?" said Mati. "Yes ... I am hungry. Now that I think of it, I doubt that I've ever been hungrier in my life."

"Good," said Lurian. Then, leaning forward, he added,

"The place of peace you went to ... it sounds beautiful. It must have been hard to leave."

Mati watched the Commander for a moment, then turned to take in Nalita and the Tygrine army. From there his eyes roved to Domino and rested on Jess. "It wasn't so hard in the end," he said. "There is no time now to live in the past – not when the future is waiting for us. And none of these lands were as precious as our own."

Epilogue

Deep within Fiåney, in the vaults of the Harakar, the phantom stalks the smoky halls. It circles them in fury and despair, stoking a fire that can never be extinguished. Lightning cracks through that haunted land, shuddering against its walls. But the spirits who dwell elsewhere in Fiåney have almost forgotten the first dark gate, the chaos that existed before Te Bubas walked the earth.

Peace unfurls in the further reaches of the dream-wake, through Sienta's limitless desert, where the first cat was born, and the meadows of Ra'ha, where her memory never fades.

Mati stands at the edge of the hilltop. The remains of a feast of warblers and larks are scattered on the sand. On his left sit Jess and Domino, with Lurian and Nalita to his right. Before them are gathered the Army of the Abyssinia Tygrine – what is left of them after years within the Boundary. Proud cats with an ancient history, with a claim for land that they have lost, and a longing to make things right again. Now they have a leader: someone to rebuild their Tygrine honour, to take back what was theirs.

Mati turns for a moment to gaze beyond the hilltop. The land is still dark, the valley tranquil. The moon has set, defeated, until the next night. "I have seen into the past," says Mati. "I have seen the great battle between the Tygrine and the Sa."

The Tygrines blink at him respectfully.

Mati continues. "It is a battle that we almost won. We were quick, and tough, and ready for combat. But the Sa Mau tricked us, used spells against us."

Several of the Tygrines hiss at such betrayal.

"We were defeated but we kept our dignity. Our fighters were brave. They never gave up hope."

The Tygrines *pirrup* and Domino joins them, eager to be part of this noble kin. Jess is quiet, watching her old friend with mixed feelings. Is this the same catling she met on the market-place, who had scarcely remembered his own name, let alone where he came from? Who had trembled before a crowd, had hated the glare of attention at his first full-moon meeting in Cressida Lock? He has changed so much; has grown stronger, and braver. She admires her friend but fears for him too, with his title and ancestry, and the burden of his legacy: his curious power to visit the dream-wake. How can she stay by his side when he runs so far ahead? How might she keep him safe?

Mati blinks at the surrounding cats. "I cannot see into the future. Unlike the past, it does not move through Fiåney's halls. Perhaps it is a world that is yet to be discovered; yet to be crafted by our words and our deeds." One ear flicks back and he looks at Jess, as though he has read her thoughts. "Do not fear loneliness there. For we shall walk that world together. Wherever it leads us, we will not be alone. Whatever it makes us, we shall always be friends." He turns back to the other cats, feeling the dizzying strength of their faith. Words that he had once struggled to find seem to flow through him, as though he is possessed by the spirit of the Tygrine lords that went before. "We are survivors, every last one of us, born to be free. A kind spirit told me that, and I shall never forget it. In liberty and kinship, we greet the future together. In fear and in danger, in joy and victory. For we are the tribe of the Tygrine, and we will triumph once more!"

Lost and alone, a young cat called Mati seeks acceptance
into the community of street cats at Cressida Lock. But Mati is
no ordinary cat … and Mithos, the mysterious assassin on his
trail, knows it. To defeat his enemies, Mati must learn to harness
an ancient feline power – a power so deadly that it threatens to
destroy not only his friends but every cat on earth.

**An award-winning fantasy about a cat
seeking his destiny**

—⁖—

"*Evidently Inbali Iserles was an Abyssinian cat in a previous existence.
She and her hero Mati share a sixth sense about feline life and she
thrills us with his daring in the face of danger.*" MARY HOFFMAN,
bestselling author of the *Stravaganza* series